BUG THE FILES

BEE-ZARRE!

DAVID JACOBS

BERKLEY BOOKS, NEW YORK

BEE-ZARRE!

A Berkley Book / published by arrangement with
the author

PRINTING HISTORY
Berkley edition / February 1997

The Putnam Berkley World Wide Web site address is
http://www.berkley.com/berkley

ISBN: 0-425-15638-9

BERKLEY®
Berkley Books are published by The Berkley Publishing Group,
200 Madison Avenue, New York, New York 10016.
BERKLEY and the "B" design
are trademarks belonging to Berkley Publishing Corporation.

PRINTED IN THE UNITED STATES OF AMERICA

10 9 8 7 6 5 4 3 2 1

BUG ᵀᴴᴱ FILES

BEE-ZARRE!

*B*ZZZZZZZZZZZZZZZ . . .

A bee buzzed around outside a window in the high-school building. On the other side of the glass sat Rita Knight, a slim brunette in this year's senior class at Sibley High School in Osbourne, Texas.

She was in a morning third-period algebra class. There were about two dozen students in the classroom. Standing at the head of the class, chalking an equation up on the blackboard, was the teacher, Mr. Chatsworth.

He was a peppery little guy who looked as if he had just bitten into a lemon. He wore horn-rimmed glasses, a bow tie, and a seersucker suit.

He chalked up the terms of the equation briskly, with short, sharp strokes. He struck the board so hard that the chalk broke in two, sending the tip shooting off at a tangent.

There was a sound of bodies stirring at their desks.

"That woke you all up, eh?" Mr. Chatsworth said, smiling sourly. The smile abruptly vanished. "Try to stay that way."

He went back to the problem, using the piece of chalk still clenched in his hand. The class resumed its daze. Some of the students went to sleep.

Rita sighed, eyeing the clock for the umpteenth time. It was early yet, the class had barely gotten started. Its end, and lunchtime, seemed a long way away.

She sat on the left side of the room, facing the board. Her desk was third from the rear in a row that ran alongside the wall. The upper two thirds of the wall was all windows, sets of glass panes in steel frames. The windowsill, about twelve inches deep, was roughly level with the desktops.

The windows opened on a west view of the school grounds and the streets beyond. The building was a long, low, rambling structure, with its long sides running north-south. It fronted west.

The algebra class was in a room on the ground floor of the south wing, facing west.

Rita sat slumped at her desk, a folded arm resting on the sill, a hand propping up her head.

On her desk lay an algebra textbook, opened to the problem now being covered by the teacher. Also a loose-leaf notebook, opened to the algebra section.

With her free hand, the one not holding up her head, Rita doodled on the notebook pages.

She glanced at the clock. Its hands seemed to be frozen at the same time they'd shown the last time she looked, just seconds ago.

She squirmed in her chair, changing position. There was a tinkling sound. She looked to see what had caused it.

On the sill, near her elbow, was a thin glass triangle, about the size of an arrowhead. The sound had come from the glass shard, when she had accidentally brushed against it with her arm.

She didn't like that so well. She looked around, to see if the sill held any more pieces of broken glass. It didn't, although there were a few crumbs of grit and flecks of what looked like dried plaster.

The glass must have come from a broken window, but at first glance, all the panes that Rita could see were intact. She looked up, from where the piece had originally lain, her gaze rising in a straight line to the top of the tall window.

There, in the uppermost row of the frame, was a cracked pane, minus a triangular-shaped piece in the corner. The missing piece matched the shard on the sill. The other debris were pieces of dried window putty.

Mystery solved. Rita eyed the damaged pane. Besides the missing piece, it had a few hairline cracks. It didn't seem in imminent danger of raining down broken glass on Rita's head.

Still, she sat up straight, taking her arm off the sill.

A bee outside the window caught her eye. It hovered at eye level, on the opposite side of the glass.

A line of shrubs bordered the front of the building, their tops reaching past the bottoms of the windows. The shrubs were overgrown with vines with green shoots and small pale bell-shaped blossoms.

The bee was buzzing around the blossoms. Occasionally it bumped against the glass. The impact didn't seem to affect it. It would bounce off, then continue buzzing around the blossoms.

A busy bee in spring in south Texas. Way south,

near the border. Outside, it was hot. Not warm—
hot. But the windows were closed. All the windows
in the school were closed. The building was air-
conditioned. All of the public buildings in this part
of the state, and almost all of the private ones,
were air-conditioned. Otherwise, the blistering
heat would make occupancy impossible for much of
the year.

Outside, it was hot. Inside, in the classroom, it
was warm. And stuffy. The air-conditioning wasn't
that great.

The bee landed on a glass pane, clinging to the
sheer vertical surface as if it were weightless. Defy-
ing gravity, it walked around in spiraling circles. It
was fingernail-sized, with dull brown and gold
bands on its body.

Abruptly, it flew off, flitting to a nearby blossom.
It crawled inside the flower, out of view.

Rita turned her gaze outward, beyond the brush
framing the bottom of the window. A square of
green lawn stretched out to the sidewalk. The
green was so fresh and bright that it looked phony,
like artificial turf, but it was real. Out back, behind
the building, the football field looked even better.

The front lawn was fenced in and off-limits. It
was split in two by a wide central walkway, which
connected the main entrance to the sidewalk and
street. The front doors were barred to students,
who had to enter and exit the building from the
side doors.

Now the students were inside, and the scene was
empty, the pavements deserted. When school was
in session, this was a quiet street, with little traffic
and few passersby. Police cars rolled through the

area regularly during school hours, stopping to question anybody loitering around the premises. If they were nonstudents, without a good reason for being there, they were told to move on. If they were students, they must be cutting classes, and were escorted inside, to the principal's office.

The town cops ran a pretty tight ship. You couldn't blame them, though. That's what the taxpayers wanted.

That's what Syntrex wanted. And Syntrex was the biggest taxpayer of all. Syntrex was the town. Without it, Osbourne, Texas, would dry up and blow away, like the rest of the towns in the county, sad flyspecks on a map of failure.

Osbourne lived in the shadow of Syntrex. Literally.

West, across the street from the high school, beyond tracts of modest single-family housing, rose the towers of Syntrex.

Rita could see them from the classroom. Osbourne was built on flat open land. The town had grown outward, expanding away from the original site. Most of the buildings were low, no more than two or three stories.

Syntrex was high. It had grown upward. It dominated the landscape.

Syntrex ChemWorks. It was an industrial plant, a titanic manufacturing complex. It made chemicals. Raw materials went in, and out came newly synthesized compounds.

Syntrex specialized in substances used in food processing. The compounds were organic, nontoxic, and biodegradable. Or at least that's what the company said. Rita's father worked there, and he said

so, too. Who knows? It might even be true, thought Rita.

The complex was a mass of storage tanks, refining towers, catwalks, and pipes. Miles of pipes, all tangled up like spaghetti, wrapping the site in a tubular web.

The towers were tall, straight, and slim, hundreds of feet high. They looked something like the oxygen tanks used in hospitals. They were sea green, the color of old copper. They weren't made of copper, but that's what color they were.

A stack near the top of a bundle of towers vented a puff of smoke. Swiftly the puff grew into a cloud. The cloud was pale yellow green. Very pale, and more yellow than green.

For a moment it clung to the towers, as if it had been spiked to their tops. Then the winds took it. They were blowing east, toward the school.

The cloud drifted, spreading, thinning, becoming a yellow-green film smeared across the sky.

Rita took little notice of it. Such ventings happened all the time, night and day. "Green Mist," the locals called it. Everybody knew about it and nobody cared. It was a by-product of the manufacturing processes. Fumes built up in the vats and had to be periodically vented. It was cheaper to blow them out of the stacks, into open air.

That was Green Mist. The winds scattered it, and the residue eventually fell to earth. It was harmless, the company said. Plenty of area ranchers and farmers had tried to prove otherwise. So had environmental activists, including some high-powered outsiders who hoped to make a test case against corporate big Syntrex.

All the tests came up zero. The stuff *was* harmless, like the company said. It was mostly water vapor, with traces of alcohol and complex organic molecules: fats, sugars, and the like.

Just then something poked Rita from behind, in the shoulder, shaking her from her daydream. She frowned, looking fierce. She looked behind her, where the poke had come from.

Behind her sat Tally Dawkins, pale, plump, with frizzy orange-red hair and sly, heavy-lidded eyes. In one hand she held a pencil, the eraser end of which had just poked Rita.

Rita gave her one of those what's-your-problem? looks. Tally, blank-faced, motioned with her head, indicating that Rita should turn her attention to the front of the room.

Rita heard her name being called and caught on too late to what Tally was trying to signal: namely that she, Rita, was being called on to answer a question by Mr. Chatsworth.

"Miss Knight!"

She faced front, flustered. "Uh, yes, Mr. Chatsworth?"

"Ah, Miss Knight. Glad you decided to join us."

"I, uh, didn't hear you." Rita's face burned. Giggles sounded among her classmates. She flashed a dirty look in their direction.

Mr. Chatsworth stood at the board, to one side of the chalked equation. He tapped a piece of chalk impatiently beside the final term of the problem.

It read: $x = ?$

"How would you solve for x, Miss Knight?" he said.

She shrugged helplessly. "I don't know."

"Well, you won't find the answer by looking out the window," he said tartly.

"Sorry," she mumbled.

Mr. Chatsworth ignored her, having made his point. "Perhaps someone would like to enlighten Miss Knight and the rest of us as to how this equation can be properly solved? Someone who's been paying attention?"

A few hands went up. The teacher called on one of their owners saying, "Go ahead, Miss Underholt, give it a try."

Lucy Underholt, small, elfin, and perky, was one of the biggest suck-ups in the whole school. She brightly began rattling off the steps of the solution.

"Couldn't you just strangle her?" Tally whispered, so only Rita could hear her. Rita nodded yes.

Something went *plink!* against the window beside her. It came from outside, a pretty solid hit that sounded like a pebble being thrown against the pane.

In fact, that's what Rita thought it was, a pebble thrown from outside, by somebody hiding below the window. Sibley HS was filled with pranksters who loved to disrupt classes.

She stared straight ahead, pointedly minding her own business. She'd already had enough trouble this morning.

Bap! Bap!

The rapping came twice, in quick succession. It was loud.

Idiot, thought Rita. Not once did the thought cross her mind that it might be somebody trying to signal her. She didn't have that many friends, and those she had knew better than to involve her in anything so public, so uncool.

Bap!-Bap!-Bap!-Bap!-Bap!

Now it sounded like someone frantically drumming fingertips against the glass pane, trying to get her attention.

She looked out the window. Tally was looking, too. Rita leaned forward, staring. The guy sitting in front of her turned around to see what was happening.

There was no one outside. No one human, that is. There was a dark, coin-sized blur hovering in midair, above the tops of the shrubbery.

It zoomed forward, launching itself headfirst against the pane of glass.

Bap!

"What *is* that?" Tally said, raspy-voiced.

"A bee," said Rita.

"He must be crazy," muttered the guy sitting in front of her.

Lucy Underholt fell silent, irked by the interruptions. She looked like a bird that had just had an egg filched out from under her in the nest.

Mr. Chatsworth stood at the head of the aisle. Behind the glasses, his eyes were almost bright. The rest of his face looked sad.

He said, "What is it now, Miss Knight?"

"I'm not doing anything," Rita said.

"It's a bug," Tally said.

"Bee," Rita corrected.

"What?" Mr. Chatsworth said.

A fresh round of bapping sounded as the blur once more beat against the glass.

The teacher, startled, said, "What's that?"

He went down the aisle, halting beside Rita's desk. He looked skeptical, as if he suspected someone of trying to put something over on him.

He peered outside, craning his neck, rising on tiptoe.

"Hmmm, I don't see anyone. . . ."

"There's nobody outside, Mr. Chatsworth," Tally said. "It's a bee."

"I don't see it."

Bap!

The bee struck the glass opposite Mr. Chatsworth's face, almost exactly at eye level.

The teacher flinched. The bee dropped, falling on the outside sill. It lay on its back, legs working feebly.

"Why, it *is* a bee," Mr. Chatsworth said. He flicked his fingers at it, making shooing motions. "It's out there, so let's get back to work."

He turned, starting up the aisle. He hadn't even reached the end of it, when there was a new outburst.

"It's back!" somebody said.

Still dazed, but making a quick recovery, the bee had righted itself and now clung to a corner of the bottom pane.

"That's one crazy bee," the guy in front of Rita said, chuckling.

"That's no bee," said a voice from across the aisle. It came from J. W. Burns, whose long lanky form was sandwiched with difficulty behind his desk. A single boyish black curl dangled over his smooth, unlined forehead.

"It's a hornet," he said.

"I believe you're wrong, J.W.," said the guy in

front of Rita, whose name was Arch Mokely. He had a blond rooster-tail haircut and wide pink lips. "It's a bee."

"I believe it's a hornet, Arch."

Burns leaned across the aisle, for a better look.

"Shoot, what's it doing now?"

The insect was spasming, clenching and un-clenching like a tiny fist. From its tail emerged a dark, wickedly curved needle point, thrusting, stab-bing.

"It's stinging the glass," Rita said, slightly unset-tled by the insect's tireless ferocity.

"I believe you're right," Burns said. "That tears it. Bees are easygoing critters, long as you don't mess with 'em. Hornets and wasps are mean. They keep coming at you. That thing's too small to be a wasp, so it must be a hornet."

"Bee," Arch Mokely said.

A new voice said, "Whatever it is, it's a mean mother."

The speaker was Albert Bray. He was wiry, with blue-black hair worn straight back, a long bony face, and shifty eyes. He was a sharp dresser.

"Look at him go," Albert said admiringly. "Man, he's dying to stick that stinger in somebody!"

Albert, Burns, and Mokely were out of their seats, grouped around Rita's desk, watching the bug. They loomed over Rita.

"Hey, guys, you mind?" she said.

"Nope," Albert said.

"You're crowding me."

"You know you love it."

"Albert, you're about to get an elbow where it hurts," she said sweetly.

He stepped back. "You'd do it, too, wouldn't you, girl?"

"You know it. And don't call me girl."

"Okay, sweet thing."

Rita groaned.

While all this was going on, Mr. Chatsworth had been standing nearby, arms folded across his chest, tapping his foot, doing a slow burn.

Nobody noticed him, so he made a few throat-clearing noises. "Ahem. Back to your seats, gentlemen. Nature-study time is over."

The others drifted toward their seats. "That's some bee," Mokely said, marveling.

"Hornet," said Burns.

Across the room, three aisles away, Lucy Underholt had her head together with Tammi Ward, one of the two main rivals in the school's beauty-queen contest. Tammi was a flawless brunette, beautiful, popular, an honor-roll student.

Seated an aisle away was the other candidate for the crown, Jean Collier. She was much like Tammi, but blond.

Jean was whispering something to her chum, Caroline Morgan, known as Caro.

Rita and Tammi made eye contact. Tammi's smile was bright. Spiteful, but bright.

"That's the most guys you've had around you all year, Rita," she said brightly.

"I'm not like you, Tammi, Little Miss Popularity."

"So they tell me."

"You should only hear what they tell me," Rita said.

Albert said, "Hey, Tammi, aren't you afraid

BEE-ZARRE!

Rita'll write something nasty about you in the school paper?"

Tammi hadn't thought of that. She wrinkled her nose, frowning. Then she brightened.

"Don't be silly," she said. "There's nothing nasty to write about because I'm not nasty. I'm nice."

". . . Yeah."

Tammi tsk-tsked. "You've got an evil mind, Albert."

"I'm nasty."

Tammi smiled at Rita. "You're a good sport, Rita. You can take a joke."

"Sure. Can you?"

Jean Collier said, just loud enough to be heard, "Tammi's running for queen is a joke."

"See how funny it is when I win the crown," Tammi said.

Mr. Chatsworth stepped in. "No politics in the classroom, please. I'll already be in enough trouble with the school board when they find out how many students are in danger of flunking this course.

"And don't make the mistake of thinking that just because you're seniors, and it's late in the school year, that grades don't matter. If you fail this course, you won't graduate! You'll have to make it up in summer school."

That sobered up some of the class, but not Albert. He nudged Burns. "Guess what, brain boy? It's a bee."

Burns thought about it, long and hard. After a while he said, "I reckon not."

"Agh! You're blind!"

Albert picked up a pen and began tapping it against the window, opposite the bee.

Tally said, "Don't get it mad!"

The bee writhed against the glass, its stinger working. A drop of venom worked out, leaving a smear.

Albert tapped at it some more with the pen. The bee batted against the window.

"You'd like to get me, wouldn't you?" Albert said, grinning.

"Albert, stop!" Tally said.

In the back row, a hulking figure sat hunched over a desk, massive arms folded on the desktop, head buried in the arms. Now the head lifted, blinking sleepily.

"Now you've done it," the teacher said. "You woke up Mr. Martens. That must be a first for this class."

"Not me," Albert said. "I didn't do it."

The waking giant was Ox Martens, a star lineman for the Sibley High football team, the Javelins. He was older than the rest of the students in class, about nineteen or twenty. Ox wasn't sure himself. He was such a good football player that the school kept holding back his graduation to get another season out of him. Not that he would have graduated anyway. This year was the last of his eligibility, so they were just going to give him a diploma and move him up and out. Graduating was part of the deal. That way, Ox could play ball for one of the half dozen or so colleges that were actively pursuing him.

He was built like a filing cabinet with big arms and legs stuck on. He had a big head, shaped like a potato. His eyes were dull and unwinking.

He said groggily, "What's all the noise?"

Mr. Chatsworth knew the score. The powers that

be at the school board had sent down the word that Ox was to be given a passing grade.

In these parts, football was taken seriously.

Mr. Chatsworth was happy to let Ox sleep away quietly in the back of the class. The arrangement suited Ox, too.

Now Ox looked puzzled. "Is the class over? I didn't hear the bell ring."

"No, Mr. Martens, the class is not over, a fact which pains me as much as it does the rest of you," the teacher said.

"So, what's going on?"

"Nothing. Nothing for you to lose any sleep over, Mr. Martens."

Ox nodded. "Okay." He put his head down on the desk, burying it in his arms.

The teacher said, "Sit down, Mr. Bray."

Albert started toward his seat. Tally said, "Hey, that's my pen!"

Albert halted, studying the pen. "Why, so it is."

Tally held out her hand. "Give it back."

He started to hand it to her, then saw the bee clinging to the window. He swatted the end of the pen against the pane.

"Gotcha!" he said.

The bee went wild, batting against the glass.

Tally grabbed back her pen. "Give me that!"

"Mr. Bray," the teacher said frostily.

Albert ducked into his seat, smirking.

Outside, the bee rose, climbing in a straight line, bumping against the windowpanes and bouncing off, still rising.

"There it goes," Albert said.

"Good riddance!" Mr. Chatsworth said, briskly

rubbing his palms together, as if he were washing his hands of the whole matter.

"There's enough pests in this class without adding any of the insect variety," he said.

The bee bounced around at the top of the frame, bumping against the pane with the triangular-shaped hole.

"Uh-oh," Rita said.

At that moment the bee flew into the room.

RITA WAS UP OUT OF HER SEAT AND HALFWAY across the room.

Burns blinked. "Wow. You sure can move fast."

The bee bobbed around under the ceiling, flying tight angry curves. It dipped, coming within a few feet of the top of Albert's head.

"Yeow!" Albert jumped up and darted to the side.

"You moved even faster than she did," Burns said.

"You'd move, too, if you had any sense, you dope!" Albert said.

"Shucks, all that fuss over one itty-bitty hornet," Burns said, smiling to himself.

"Bee," said Mokely.

The class was unsettled. Mr. Chatsworth held up his hands, trying to quell the excitement.

"Let's not get hysterical, people," the teacher called out over the rising murmurs of unease.

"It's just a bee, for Pete's sake," he said. "Leave it alone, and it'll leave you alone—*yikes!*"

He choked off his words as the bee dove toward his head. He ducked. It missed, whizzing past.

It looped the loop, the high arc of its circling barely missing one of the overhead light fixtures. It slowed, dropped, then hovered in midair.

Its buzzing sounded like an electric toothbrush.

Mr. Chatsworth crouched in the aisle, down on one knee, clutching the side of a desk. The class was silent, motionless. Everyone held their breath.

Somebody breathed, "It's trying to decide who to go after. . . ."

Ox Martens stirred, lifting his head. He was groggy, bleary-eyed. "Noisy today."

Drawn by sound and motion, the bee flew to him. It landed on the top of his head, its buzzing silenced.

Ox didn't know what had happened. He felt something crawling around on his head. He brushed it off with a swipe of his pawlike hand.

It landed on the back of his neck and crawled inside his collar.

Even Ox could sense that something was wrong. He said, "How come everybody's looking at me?"

Suddenly Ox spasmed. He went rigid. His shoulders hunched. His face widened, thick features swelling, reddening. He looked like he was being compressed by heavy gravity.

He roared, bee-stung.

The bee struck again and again. Ox stood up, bellowing, knocking over his desk. It fell on its side in the aisle. Ox beat on his back with his hands, as if he were trying to beat out a fire. The bee was somewhere in the loose folds of his shirt behind his back. He couldn't get at it, but it was getting to him.

All the time, he kept bellowing. He had plenty of lung power and he wasn't holding back.

He staggered backward, into the wall. He slammed his back into the wall, trying to crush the stinging bee. It sounded like a wet fish being slapped down on a butcher's board. He did it again and again. He did it so hard that a wall bracket holding a bunch of rolled-up charts fell off and hit him on the head.

He tore off his shirt, ripping it like tissue paper, tearing it off his back. The sight of his bare torso, all that heaving flesh, was especially shocking in a classroom setting.

He slapped at his back, fingers closing on something. He crushed it. He held the hand in front of him. The bellowing had stopped and he was panting, sobbing for breath. His face was bright red, wet with tears and snot.

Pinched between his fingertips was a mashed dark blot with a few quivering wirelike feelers.

"I've got you, you dirty little so-and-so," Ox said.

The thing stung him again. Ox howled, dropping it.

It lay on the floor, twitching.

Nursing his wounded fingers by tucking them under an arm, Ox stomped the bee with one of his big size-twelve boots. He stomped it so hard that he broke through the floorboards.

"IT KEPT COMING . . . STINGING AND STINGING," Ox said, sniffling.

His back was marked with a clump of what looked like boils, each inflicted by a separate sting. They were bright red. So was much of the skin surrounding them. There was a broad patch of redness on the back of his shoulders and between his shoulder blades. The rest of his skin was pasty white.

Mr. Chatsworth said, "Are you allergic to bee stings, Mr. Martens?"

"No. I've been stung before. Not like that. It just kept coming."

"We'd better get you to the infirmary."

"Why me? Why'd it pick on me?"

The door opened, and two teachers stuck their heads in: Mrs. Hanford, a history teacher; and Mr. Pitney, an English teacher. Their classrooms were nearby.

"What's all the ruckus?" Mr. Pitney said.

Mrs. Hanford gasped. "Heavens!"

"This young man was stung by a bee," Mr. Chatsworth said, indicating Ox.

The newcomers stared in disbelief.

"He was stung a number of times. A severe attack. It's quite serious," Mr. Chatsworth said, solemn-faced.

Ox started. He put a hand to his throat. "Serious? What do you mean, serious? Tell me the truth, how bad off *am* I?"

Ox grabbed the teacher's shoulder with his good hand, the one that hadn't been stung. "How bad am I? *Am I gonna die?*"

"I'd like to keep the arm if you don't mind, Mr. Martens," the teacher said, wincing.

Ox let go.

"Thank you," Mr. Chatsworth said. He worked his shoulder around, trying to get some feeling back where Ox had gripped it.

"That's better, I can feel the numbness going away," he said. "No, Mr. Martens, you're not going to die. A healthy specimen like you won't succumb to a few bee stings, no matter how painful."

Ox nodded, grunting. Mr. Chatsworth studied him, saying, "You're sure you're not allergic?"

"No . . . I don't know." The trapped look came back to Ox's eyes. "What difference does it make anyhow?"

"None, I'm sure."

"You don't sound sure."

"Nonsense." Mr. Chatsworth turned to the other teachers, who had entered the room and stood near the door.

"I'm going to take Mr. Martens to the infirmary. Will one of you watch the class, please?"

"Certainly, Mr. Chatsworth."

"Thank you, Mr. Pitney."

Mr. Chatsworth placed a hand on Ox's arm. it was like gripping a tree branch. With the lightest of touches, he guided Ox across the room, steering him toward the door.

Ox shuffled along, head down, like a zombie. Mr. Pitney and Mrs. Hanford moved aside to let him pass.

Mrs. Hanford started, staring. "My goodness! He's so red in the face!"

The redness extended from Ox's hairline to a point between his shoulder blades, like a skintight hood.

"That *is* serious," Mrs. Hanford said in a loud stage whisper, holding a hand to her mouth.

"Agh!" Ox cried, spooked.

"Tut-tut," Mr. Chatsworth said. He was the kind of guy who could say "tut-tut" and get away with it.

"Tut-tut, Mrs. Hanford, surely not as serious as all that. Not serious at all. A bee-sting case. Routine. Happens all the time," Mr. Chatsworth said, speaking with forced cheeriness.

He patted Ox's shoulder encouragingly. "This young man's had a painful experience and a bad scare. Let's not add to it. A positive mental attitude, that's what's needed. Don't you agree, Mr. Pitney?"

"Absolutely, Mr. Chatsworth."

Ox chewed the corner of his lips, glazed eyes staring. He started breathing hard.

"I feel funny," he said.

"You'll be fine. Won't he, Mr. Pitney?"

"Absolutely, Mr. Chatsworth."

"But we'd better get Mr. Martens to the infirmary."

"Immediately," Pitney said.

The two of them got Ox in motion again, shepherding him toward the exit. Mrs. Hanford watched them go by. She stood with her hands on her hips, shaking her head.

"He looks bad to me," she said.

"Ohh," Ox said. His eyes went wide and his knees went wobbly. He stumbled, lurching into the door, nearly taking it off the hinges.

"Whoops!" Mr. Chatsworth said. "Careful there, Mr. Martens!"

"I'm okay." Ox's sickly smile was awful to see. "I've been hit worse than this plenty of times on the line."

"I'm sure," Mr. Chatsworth said. He got on one side of Ox, and Mr. Pitney got on the other. They each took hold of an arm.

Ox flinched. "Watch out for my bad hand." The fingers that had been stung were swollen like sausage links. He held the hand out in front of him.

"Okay, let's go," he said. He shuffled off, flanked by the two teachers. They held him by the arms, steering him. He moved under his own power. They turned, crossing to the south stairwell at the end of the hall.

Mrs. Hanford stood in the doorway, her back to the room, watching them go.

The class was beginning to recover from its shocked immobility.

Tally tried to speak, but her voice cracked. She swallowed hard and tried again. "That was too weird!"

"Bee-zarre," Rita said.

ALBERT LAUGHED SHAKILY. "GOOD THING football season's over."

"Very funny," Lucy said, unamused. "It wouldn't have happened if you hadn't gotten that bee riled up."

"Watch your mouth," Albert said sharply. He lightened up his tone. "People might not know you're kidding and get the wrong idea."

Mrs. Hanford stepped back inside, closing the door. She was a dried-up stick figure with a mop of brassy blond curls. She folded her arms across the top of her bony chest.

"Bee, my eye! I'd like to know what really went on here," she said.

Student voices chorused, protesting. It *was* true, a lone bee had blitzed Ox Martens. But Mrs. Hanford couldn't be budged.

"I've been teaching for over twenty years, and in that time I've dealt with spider bites, snakebites, scorpion stings, and, yes, bee stings," she began.

"Man! Did all that happen here at Sibley?" somebody said.

"No," she said, irked at the interruption. "It happened at a number of different schools that I've worked at over the years."

"The whole county's infested," Burns said.

"I never doubted it," said Mokely. "Or maybe it's just the places where Miz Hanford worked."

"Could be," Burns said.

Mrs. Hanford glared in their direction. "It doesn't matter where I've worked. The point is that I've handled lots of emergencies involving insect bites, and I've never seen one bee do that much damage."

"Maybe it was a hornet," Arch Mokely said.

Burns said, "Sounds like you're changing your tune there, Arch."

"Well, J.W., I've been studying on the matter, and it appears to me that you're right. Everybody knows a bee can only sting once, or at the most twice, before dying. Hornet keeps on stinging you. The way that bug took after ol' Ox, it must've been a hornet."

"That's funny. I got a good look at it when it landed on Ox, and I have to admit, it sure looked like a bee to me."

Mrs. Hanford said, "All I know is, it's all mighty mysterious." She raised an eyebrow, trying to look shrewd and skeptical. It made her look cockeyed.

"There's one kind of bee that can sting many times," Rita said, thinking out loud. "Killer bees."

"What an imagination," Albert sneered. "You ought to write for one of those supermarket tabloids."

"No, no, she's right! Killer bees!" Caro said, really connecting with the idea. She fidgeted in her seat,

more excited than afraid. Her eyes shone, there
was color in her cheeks. She clapped her hands
once.

"Killer bees! That's it," she said.

"What do you think, J.W.? Reckon it was a killer
bee?"

"Could be, Arch."

"Could be a killer bee."

"Could be."

Lucy said, "Killer bee—that's ridiculous!"

Caro rose to the challenge. "What do *you* think it
was?"

"A bee, Caro, a plain old bee."

"Hah! Tell that to Ox."

Lucy gave her head a sassy little toss. "You're so
dramatic, Caro. You're always trying to make a
three-ring circus out of everything."

"That's how she's running Jean's campaign,"
Tammi said, behind her hand, but loud enough to
be heard.

"What're you running? A freak show?" Caro said.

"Play nice, girls," somebody said.

"Let 'em fight," Albert said. "Maybe somebody's
blouse will get torn and we'll see something."

Rita said, "You'd like that, huh, Albert?"

"Who wouldn't? Yum-yum!"

"You're such a pig," she said, not hostile, merely
stating a fact.

"I know. Ain't I great?"

"No."

Mrs. Hanford said, "Settle down, class."

Caro said, "How can we settle down, when we've
just seen a killer bee attack?"

"Don't go starting rumors, Caro. You don't know that it's a killer bee."

"But, Mrs. Hanford—"

The teacher cut her off with a short chopping hand gesture. "Besides, there are no killer bees in this county."

"They found a couple of hives in Ventralia last year," somebody said.

"That's in the next county," Mrs. Hanford said, smug.

"Just over the county line."

"That's still in the next county."

"A couple of kids got stung pretty near to death last month camping on the Chochoya."

"It was never proved that those were killer bees."

"The kids drifted miles downriver in a canoe. That's why they couldn't find the hive."

"That's a long way from here."

"Not that long, Miz Hanford. The river runs right through town."

"I meant the campsites. They're ten miles away."

"Seven, actually."

"My, you are persistent. Perhaps you'd like to write a five-thousand-word report on the subject."

"No ma'am."

"Then you'd better stop spreading fantastic rumors," she said. "And that goes for the rest of the class."

Lucy flashed Caro one of those that-shows-you glances. Caro's manic mood was undiminished, however, leaving her unable to sit still.

"I can't wait to spread the news!" she whispered to Jean.

The class settled down somewhat, waiting out

the clock for the end of the period. The time for the bell neared, but Mr. Chatsworth did not return. There was no word of Ox.

At last the bell rang. The class was up on its feet, rushing the door. Mrs. Hanford seemed as eager as the rest to quit the room. They streamed into the hall.

As he was passing behind Mrs. Hanford's back Albert cupped a hand over his mouth, pinched his nostrils shut, and went "Bzzzzzzzzzzzzzzzzzzzzzzz!"

It sounded pretty realistic. Mrs. Hanford jumped, and so did some students, males and females. There were a few screeches.

Albert lowered his hand and played along, looking as surprised as everybody else.

Under his breath, he said, "Suckers."

They weren't to blame. They had a right to be spooked. They had seen what a bee could do. Mrs. Hanford hadn't witnessed the attack, but she'd seen the results, tattooed in pain on Ox's hide.

A bee had done that. One lone bee. A killer bee.

There were more on the way. Many more.

And soon.

THE WIND CHANGED DIRECTION. BEFORE, IT HAD been blowing into the east. Now, it shifted, blowing first to the southeast, then south. It wasn't much of a wind, not really. More of a stiff breeze. Still, it did the job, sweeping airborne particles of Green Mist before it.

At twenty minutes to noon, Deke Garland exited the machine-parts store. He was a middle-aged ranch hand. He was thin, tough, and leathery, like beef jerky. He held a box containing the tractor-engine part for which he'd come into town.

The parts store was about a half mile southeast of the high school. It sat on a lot on the west side of the highway, which ran north-south. The highway was one of the main roads in south Texas. It ran through the center of Osbourne, where it became Main Street. Outside of town, it became the highway again.

The parts store was south of the town plaza and the business district, where both sides of the highway were lined with convenience stores, fast-food franchises, and mini-malls.

Outside, it was hot and hazy. The air had a kind of oily sheen and there was a smell of banana oil. A chemical smell, fruity, too sweet.

Green Mist. Nobody around that didn't know that smell, Garland thought. He glanced at the plant, which was easily visible at this distance, as it was from most places on the flats. No smoke blew from the stacks. The venting must have been done earlier, while he was in the parts store.

He went to his vehicle, a sporty low-slung pickup truck. It wasn't his. He only drove it on ranch errands. It belonged to his boss.

He got in. The windows were rolled down but it was hot anyway. He placed the box on the seat beside him.

He fired up the engine. The windshield was dulled by a green-tinged film. He spritzed it with the windshield washer. Wipers cleaned the screen, leaving behind faint ghostly rainbow swirls.

He turned on the radio. It was set to a country-music station. The air conditioner was broken. No relief there. That's why the windows were down.

He got on the highway south, driving out of town. There was a fair amount of traffic, big rig trucks, delivery vans, cars.

It was lunch hour. The parking lots of the fast-food joints were filling up fast.

Once he passed the end of the strip, the road was clear. He stepped on the gas and drove faster. As noontime neared he was a few miles south of town.

Out here, there were few buildings and much land. A handful of structures dotted the roadside:

general stores, gas stations, roadhouses, produce stands. They pressed up close to the roadway. Beyond lay vast fields, farms, ranches. Some of the fields were bright squares of green-growing things, thanks to irrigation.

Ahead, flashing red lights warned of a railroad crossing. The crossing was in use. The set of railroad tracks met the highway at right angles. A freight train rolled down the line, heading east toward the not-too-distant Gulf coast.

It wasn't a long one, as freight trains went. Garland could see the end of it. He pulled up at the crossing, behind the safety line. Black-and-white-striped poles were down, barring the way.

Red lights flashed. Warning bells clanged. The train rumbled, steam whistle sounding as an endless line of boxcars slid past.

Garland waited. The engine idled. So did he.

On his right, a drainage ditch ran alongside the road. In it flowed a muddy green stream. The sides of the ditch were weedy. A tunnel ran under the bottom of the railroad embankment, allowing the stream to flow freely to the other side.

The tunnel mouth was a black-green disk, two feet wide. The sun was overhead, but bushes kept much of the stream in the shade, filtering out all but a few rays.

From out of the brush overhanging the ditch rose a cloud of bees. One instant they weren't there, the next instant they were. Or so it seemed. Actually, they had been there all the time, buzzing the plants, seeking nectar, foraging for the hive, which was nearby. They liked the cool shade by the water.

They hated the storm of noise and smoke and mo-

tion that was the train. It brutalized them, hammering their nervous systems.

But there was something in the air that was stronger than all these things: the scent of death.

The scent that says *kill*.

Not *says*. Commands.

Having received the command, the bees could do nothing but obey. Being killer bees, they were made for mayhem.

They flew in a globe-shaped formation, a blurry, free-flowing shape. There was a core group of about a hundred bees, with more arriving every second.

Garland didn't see them. He was too busy watching the train go by. They buzzed, but the sound was drowned out by the train.

They flew in the windows, swarming him. They were Hive. He was not-Hive: *Enemy!*

They hit him like a biblical plague, stinging his eyes, nose, face, flying in his screaming mouth, stinging there, too. A cloud of evil imps, hammering red-hot needles into his flesh.

Poison needles, pumping him full of brain-blasting venom.

He opened the door and attempted to get out. There were more bees outside, oblivious to the train rushing past less than a dozen feet away. The air wash from the train's passage didn't reach them.

Garland fell back into the cab. It was full of bees. Their buzzing sounded like a power saw. The madder they got, the higher-pitched it got.

Now it was a dentist's drill, boring into his nerve ends.

Escape! He had to get away, get to a doctor—

He threw the truck into gear, stepped on the gas.

He meant to throw it into reverse, but he couldn't see, and he couldn't think, either. He flailed away at the controls until he threw it into something, then gave it the gas.

By mistake he'd thrown it into drive.

The vehicle lunged forward, like an overeager runner getting a false start off the starting block. It snapped the zebra-striped gate bars and rammed into the side of the train.

Tortured metal howled. The stricken boxcar shuddered, its side caving in. But it was not derailed. It stayed on track.

The front of the pickup truck crumpled, accordioning. The engine was shoved back into the cab, filling it. The steering column thrust out through the cab's rear window.

Somewhere in there was Garland, now Garland-no-more. Massive trauma meant instant death.

The front of the pickup hooked onto the side of the train, dragging the vehicle sideways alongside the track. Glass showered, sparks spewed, gas and oil spurted as the machine was dragged to destruction. The noise sounded like a riot in Heavy-Metal Hell.

The wreck was hauled about fifty yards down the line before it fell off. It pinwheeled, tearing off some more pieces of itself before finally rolling to a halt.

AFTER LUNCH, RITA'S NEXT CLASS WAS BIOLogy. The teacher was Mr. Huff. He had thinning brown hair and wore a brown suit and tie. A handful of students in the class had been present during the attack on Ox, and were giving the others their eyewitness accounts until Mr. Huff called a halt to the chatter and began teaching the lesson.

About ten minutes into the period, the public-address system came to life. This classroom, like all the others, was equipped with a wall-mounted intercom-type speaker, allowing messages to be broadcast from the PA apparatus in the school's administrative office.

There were some electronic cracklings, followed by a feedback squeal. Then came the message, simultaneously broadcast throughout the building:

"Attention, students. This is a special announcement. This is Vice-Principal Brock speaking," it began.

The mention of Brock's name set off some boos,

jeers, and hisses. "All right, class, knock it off," Mr. Huff said.

Brock continued: *"As some of you know, a student was injured earlier today. It appears that he was stung by some kind of flying insect. He was treated by Emergency Service paramedics and is doing fine. I'm sure that you will join Principal Twonky, myself, and the rest of the faculty and staff in wishing him a speedy return to school.*

"I urge all students to resist the fear-mongering and sensationalized accounts that have already begun to surround this admittedly unfortunate incident. Repeating fantastic and untrue stories about the event is a blow to school spirit. With Founder's Day coming up, there are many positive activities to focus on. Let's concentrate on them. Say no to negativity.

"At the same time, students are reminded to use caution when confronted with insect pests. Sibley High School is a bug-free environment, but accidents do happen. Insects can inflict painful bites and stings. If you see such insects, do not molest them. Instead, bring them to the attention of the nearest faculty member. Do not try to dispose of them yourselves.

"That is all. This is Vice-Principal Brock. Good day and—good grades."

The speaker hum faded, cutting out with a few last electronic bleeps and blats.

"Even the speaker is giving ol' Brocky the raspberry," somebody said.

Albert said, "Hey, Mr. Huff, if I see any bugs, I'm not going to molest them. I'll leave them for you to molest."

"Don't *interfere* with them, Albert. That's what the vice-principal meant."

"Oh. I was wondering."

Caro's arm shot up, raising her hand. Not waiting to be called on, she blurted, "Mr. Huff! Do you think it was a killer bee that attacked Ox?"

"I don't know, Caro. I wasn't there."

"But what do you think?"

"I think we should do as Mr. Brock says, and not start up any rumors."

"I was there, Mr. Huff! I saw it! It stung him about twelve times!"

"Six, anyway," Rita said.

"It stung him a lot of times. That's what a killer bee does," Caro said.

"How can you tell a killer bee from a regular one?" asked somebody else.

"That's enough killer-bee talk," Mr. Huff said.

"This is a biology class," Rita said. "If we can't talk about it here, where can we talk about it?"

"I thought that's what science is all about," Caro said.

"If I open my mouth on the subject," the teacher said, "the next thing you know, everybody will be saying that 'Mr. Huff says it's a killer bee.' Then I'll be the one called down to Mr. Brock's office to explain myself. Didn't you hear what he said?"

"I try not to," somebody said.

"On the other hand," Mr. Huff went on, "the best way to fight rumors is with the truth. I don't think Mr. Brock could object to that. I refuse to comment on today's incident, but I will make a few general remarks about so-called killer bees.

"I say 'so-called' because killer bees are really

just another strain of common honeybees. They
originally came from sub-Saharan Africa, a harsh
desert climate. As a result, they're more aggressive and territorial than their cousins from the
more temperate northern regions. It's a result of
climate. Species of termites and ants from the
area are also far fiercer than their counterparts
from other regions.

"The sub-Saharan species is not only aggressive,
it's well armed. The common-variety bee usually
can only sting once. Its sting is fatal to itself. When
it stings, the stinger is torn off, along with much of
the bee's abdomen, causing death.

"Not the sub-Saharan bee. Its stinger does not
tear off. It can sting many times without injuring
itself. That's what makes it so dangerous. That,
and its fierce territoriality.

"Other bees attack when the hive is directly
threatened. The sub-Saharan variety attacks when
an intruder is in the vicinity of a hive. The victim
may not even know that there's a hive nearby, until
the bees are on him. By then, it's too late."

A student said, "How'd they get here, Mr. Huff?"

"Sometime back in the 1960s, a strain was
brought to Brazil. Beekeepers tried to crossbreed
the sub-Saharans with a domestic South Ameri-
can bee. They wanted to introduce some of that
sub-Saharan physical hardiness into the domestic
strain.

"Instead, they got a hybrid with all of the fierce-
ness of the imported strain, that was better
adapted to local conditions thanks to the domestic
strain.

"What they had was a menace. Unfortunately,

the bees somehow got loose. They spread rapidly, too fast to be stopped. Where they found hives of domestic bees, they drove them out.

"The species is very successful. It's been expanding, migrating up through Central America and Mexico. Yes, and Texas. There've been a few recorded incidents in the state, not many. None in Osbourne.

"There's a lot of hysteria about killer bees. But their attacks on humans are a lot rarer than you'd think, judging from the scare headlines and trash-TV shows.

"For you students, the chance of being attacked by killer bees is infinitely small, compared to the risk of being in a fatal auto crash or a shooting. Or of dying from smoking-related illnesses," Mr. Huff said.

"It sure looked like a killer-bee attack to me!"

"You said that, Caro, not me. I didn't see what happened, so I'm not going to express an opinion on the subject. That's the scientific way.

"I will say that I think it's highly unlikely that we're in any danger from killer bees," the teacher said, smiling thinly to show just how ridiculous the idea was.

"If there's any meaning to be found in this whole unhappy business, it's that biology isn't just something that's found in textbooks," Mr. Huff concluded "It's part of the world around us. Sometimes it can reach out and sting you. So, be careful about what you go around stirring up."

"Especially if it's a killer bee," Rita said.

"No more killer-bee talk," Mr. Huff said. He went back to teaching the assigned lesson.

Under her breath, eyes wide, chin stubbornly set, Caro said, "I know it's killer bees, I just know it!"

If the teacher heard her, he let it pass.

"CRAZY FOOL DROVE HEAD-ON INTO THE SIDE of the train!" the engineer said, shaken. He had a weathered freckled face and pale, almost invisible eyebrows. He stood near the locomotive, talking to Sheriff Dell.

"Did you see it happen?" the sheriff said.

"No. I saw the truck standing at the crossing. Didn't think anything of it. Then there was a noise and I looked back and saw that we were dragging the truck, what was left of it. I stopped the train. The truck broke loose, rolled, and burned," the engineer said.

He wiped his sweaty forehead in the elbow of his shirt. Fresh sweat beaded up in its place. Under the sweat he was pale.

The train stood idle, occupying a curved length of track about an eighth of a mile long. It was a freight train, with no passengers. The crew stood around the train, on the side of the crash. Midway along its length was the damaged boxcar. Its side was caved in, but the undercarriage and wheels seemed more or less intact.

The wrecked truck lay in a ditch beside the railroad embankment. It had flipped over, a burned-out hulk. The metal was still hot and the melted tires still smoldered. Circling it were patches of burned ground and some small fires.

The site was in the middle of a wide stretch of empty open ground. In the distance were low rounded brown hills.

On the other side of the ditch, opposite the train, was a level area where some vehicles were parked. There were a couple of official sheriff's department cars, a paramedic emergency van, a fire truck, and one or two unmarked cars belonging to civil agency investigators.

Grouped around them were uniformed county deputies, paramedics, firefighters, and investigators.

A line of smoke rose from the wreck. The road leading to the railroad crossing was closed, blocked at its head by a police car. A number of cars and trucks lined the highway, filled with the curious. Deputies tried to move them along, but the gaping spectators kept progress to a crawl.

Sheriff Lloyd Dell was one of the new breed of Texas law-enforcement officers. He was trim, businesslike, and college-educated. He looked like he could have been an oil-company executive or a hard-nosed city manager. He was part politician, a successful vote getter. The citizens of the county had recently elected him to his first term as sheriff.

Above all, he was tough. That was the quality that the citizens valued most in a lawman. Without that toughness, the rest was just hype.

He had a craggy face, bushy eyebrows. He wore civilian clothes, a tan hat, brown suit, and cowboy boots. He wore aviator-style sunglasses with orange lenses. He glanced at the engineer, who was wringing his hands.

"What a terrible thing!" the engineer wailed.

"Terrible," said Sheriff Dell.

"Why did it have to happen to me? Now I'm late, and I'll be stuck here for hours longer. There goes my record for always getting the freight through on time!"

"Slow down. *He* was in a hurry, and look where it got him," Dell said, indicating the wreck.

"In a hurry to get himself killed! Only why'd he have to pick my train to do it?"

The sheriff frowned. "That's what I'd like to know."

A deputy crossed to the edge of the rise, gesturing for Dell to come up. Dell climbed up the side of the ditch, joining the other.

The deputy was Lex Winters, a high-ranking senior member of the department. He had slitted blueberry-colored eyes and a silver walrus mustache. He wore a brown-and-tan uniform, a badge, and a gun.

He said, "Sorry to get you up here, Lloyd, but I thought you'd better see this."

He pointed in the opposite direction, toward the highway, where a Jeep-type vehicle was driving the wrong way along the near shoulder of the roadway.

It turned onto the field and started up the slope, kicking up dust. The surprise tactic had put it beyond the reach of the patrol cars guarding the area.

"This site is off-limits!" Dell said angrily. "Who is that? Never mind. I recognize the vehicle. There's only one like it in the county."

"Mr. Larry," Winters said.

"That's right, Lex, Mr. Larry."

"There's only one of him in the county, too."

"That could be one too many," Dell said. He tilted back his hat, put his hands on his hips, and glared down at the oncoming vehicle.

It was still a long way off. It was a big field.

A young deputy stood beside a parked patrol car, holding a radio handset. "What'll we do, Sheriff?"

"Let him come."

The young deputy spoke into the handset. "The sheriff says let him come."

A garbled transmission came crackling through the car radio. The young deputy translated: "The boys on the road say they're sorry, Sheriff, but he sneaked through and they didn't see him coming—"

"Never mind the excuses," Dell said. "Tell them to make sure it doesn't happen again. No unauthorized persons get through that line. If they try, arrest them!"

"Yes, sir!"

"And that goes double for any of Larry Hummel's people. If they get tough, use any force necessary to apprehend them. That's a direct order!"

"Hooray—I mean, yessir, Sheriff!"

The Jeep was halfway across the field. It was a low-slung, open-topped, rugged four-wheel-drive

utility vehicle. It was painted with a tan-and-brown desert-camouflage pattern. In it were two people, a young female driver and a male passenger.

Some of the deputies had moved away from the cars and now stood grouped in a loose line, facing the newcomers. They stood around too casually, hands hooked into their gun belts, rocking back on their heels, whistling aimlessly.

"Looks like the boys are ready for trouble, Lloyd."

"There won't be any trouble, Rex. Tell them to break it up and go on back to what they were doing," the sheriff said.

Winters crossed to the others and gave them the word. They drifted away. He stood beside Dell.

"What is that, Rex, some kind of fancy Jeep?"

"Kind of, but lower, with a wider wheelbase."

"Military style."

"Safari Range Rover, is what he calls it. Or something. Anyhow, it's all legal, down to the paperwork."

"Trust Mr. Larry for that!" Dell grinned, his upper lip curling. "We'll never take him on the small stuff. He's too smart for that. No, when he finally slips up, it'll be something big."

Winters glanced meaningfully toward the wreck. "Like that?"

"I wonder," Dell said.

The Range Rover topped the rise and steered toward Dell and Winters, jerking to a halt about six feet away from them.

Dust clouds settled around the vehicle. It could now be seen that the woman was young and the man old; the latter was the celebrated Mr. Larry.

Winters started forward, checking himself in mid-stride as Dell said, "Hold it."

Winters looked questioningly at him.

"Mr. Larry can come to us," the sheriff said.

THERE WAS EXCITEMENT IN THE AIR, EVEN MORE than was usual at this time during weekdays, when the last bell sounded the end of the school day. And that was plenty exciting.

Rita's last class was on the second floor. Her locker was on the first floor, north of the front entrance. By the time she reached her locker and began dialing the combination, other students were already on their way out the doors.

The side doors, that is. The main entrance was off-limits to students. The doors weren't locked, that would have been a fire hazard, a violation of safety rules. But they were off-limits nonetheless. Most days, Mr. Brock stood guard beside them, as if daring any student who was bold or careless enough to try, just try, to use the forbidden doors.

Today, no Brock. It had been a hectic day, what with the insect attack and all, and the vice-principal had other, more pressing duties to attend to.

But it wasn't the absence of Brock that prompted a sudden rush of students out the front door.

What *was* it? Rita looked, seeing only exiting students.

Fighting the outgoing tide was a figure attempting to move in the opposite direction, to enter, a medium-sized shapely brunette with big round glasses.

This was Stephanie, Rita's close friend. She motioned urgently, signaling Rita to join her.

"Come on! Lucy and Caro are getting into it outside!" she called.

Rita abandoned her locker and crossed quickly to her friends. "This I *have* to see! Are they fighting, Steff?"

"Not yet, but it looks promising!"

The two squeezed into the crowd and exited. Outside, it was hot and sticky, overcast. The sun was a pale disk swimming behind the featureless gray dome of the sky. The air was thick, still.

The wide central walkway connecting the main entrance with the street was packed with about a hundred students. At both ends of the building, more students were exiting, pouring onto the sidewalk fronting the street, working from both ends to the middle. Lined along the curb was a row of yellow school buses, doors open and waiting.

As yet, few if any of the students were aware of the scene developing in the central walkway. But a cluster like that usually meant a fight, and they were picking up the vibes. The knot of onlookers seemed more curious and amused than excited, which meant that so far it wasn't much of a fight.

Stephanie said, "Brocky will have a fit when he sees how many kids are using his precious front doors."

"Yes, but there's too many for him to do anything about it," Rita said.

Stephanie's brown eyes were wide behind her glasses. "What a day! First Ox, and now this! Wild, huh?"

"Bee-zarre."

Stephanie looked sharply at her. "Not you, too! I've been hearing that corny pun all day!"

"I said it first," Rita claimed.

"Shame on you," said Stephanie.

While they were talking the two edged their way through the crowd, toward the center. Since nothing had happened yet, they were able to reach the inner ring without much difficulty.

In the center was an open space, where Lucy and Caro faced off. The two stood eye to eye, with a few feet between them. Grouped about each opponent were the core members of their rival cliques. Lucy was sided by Tammi and three of her followers, and Caro was sided by Jean and a few of her closest girlfriends.

It was hardly a catfight, though. More like a kitten fight. But you never knew: Caro and Lucy were just getting warmed up.

Lucy was preparing to deliver her Sunday punch. You could tell from the expression on her face that she thought it would be a beaut.

"You know what your trouble is, Caro? You don't have any school spirit," Lucy taunted. "All you're doing with that killer-bee talk is trashing our school!"

That got some approving nods from those among the watchers who were inclined to follow the rules. This group was not overlarge.

"Lucy, you trash the school every time you open your mouth," Caro said.

"Ooh," somebody said.

"Oh, that's great," Lucy said. "That really shows some school spirit." She was smiling now.

Caro spoke beyond her, to the onlookers. "The best linemen in the county couldn't stop Ox. Are you trying to tell me that he could be flattened by an ordinary bee?"

That produced some head nodding. "It'd take a tank to stop Ox," somebody said.

"If that," added another.

Now it was Caro's turn to smile, her eyes glittering. "It'd take a super-bee, a killer bee!"

"You are so sick," Lucy said. "But the one I'm really surprised at is you, Jean."

At the mention of her name, Jean glanced at Lucy, a mere flick of the eyes, cool and measured.

Jean's hair was so blond it was almost white. Every strand was in place, forming a platinum helmet. Her complexion was so bright and clear that it shone.

"Did you say something, Lucy?" Jean crooned, her voice low, clear, and musical. It carried a note of lazy amusement that made Lucy's face redden.

Tammi put a hand on Lucy's shoulder. Lucy leaned forward, red-faced.

She said, "You've got some nerve running for the crown, Jean, while your best friend Caro goes around sliming our school with her crazy talk! Or do you feel that way, too?"

"Tell us, Jean! I think we've all got a right to know before we vote for the girl who can best repre-

sent our school as Javelina Queen in front of the whole town on Founders' Day!"

"I'm sure that our fellow students will make the right choice," Jean said, smiling.

"I'm sure they will," Tammi echoed, just as sweetly. She and Jean acknowledged each other with slight nods.

"Yuck," Stephanie commented, making a face. "Doesn't it make you sick?"

Rita nodded. "Jean's really good. Did you see the way she blushed?"

"Yes! How does she do that?"

"She can blush at will. She's been able to do it ever since grade school."

"Tammi's slick, too. I know you don't like her, but you've got to give her that."

"I'd like to give her a swift kick," Rita said.

The scene was winding down. "No fight," somebody said, disappointed.

"Let's go, I don't want to miss the bus," said another.

Lucy couldn't resist the urge to sum up the aborted confrontation. "I guess we know who's got the school spirit around here!"

"Buzz off," Caro said.

That got a laugh.

"It runs in the family," Lucy said tightly. "Your mother was in the nuthouse, Caro, wasn't she?"

Ooh.

"At least she wasn't in the doghouse, Lucy. That's where your mother came from."

Ahh.

Caro said, "That's why you're such a b—"

"Brock!" somebody shouted. "Here comes Brock!"

The crowd began to disperse fast, onlookers moving away from the school. From out of the front doors marched the vice-principal of Sibley High School, Bennett Brock.

He was short, stocky, and bald, his skull utterly hairless. He was clean-shaven, but with a premature five o'clock shadow. He wore a dark gray suit, white shirt, and skinny black tie. In his jacket breast pocket was a plastic protective pen holder, lined with a row of pens.

He stepped out onto the walk, glaring out from under a heavy brow line, arms at his side, each arm taking a tight swing of no more than eighteen inches per stride, the soles of his shiny black shoes slapping the pavement.

He stopped, outraged. "These doors are off-limits!"

The students kept moving in the opposite direction, fast, not looking back. A few eager beavers drifted off the pavement and onto the lawn, trying to outdistance the others.

"Keep off the grass!" Brock shouted.

A handful of stragglers and slow-wits lagged behind, near the main entrance. Some had frozen in place at the first sound of Brock's voice.

He rounded them up and herded them toward the door. "Get back in that building and go out the right way, through the side doors!"

They got, glad to escape Brock's wrath so easily.

The others, the great majority who'd kept on going, mixed with the mass of students crowding the sidewalk.

Rita found herself alongside Tammi.

"This could be the deciding issue in the election,

Tammi. What's your position on the killer-bee question?"

Tammi's reply was short and unsweet.

"I can't print that!" Rita said cheerfully.

"Drop dead."

"That's better, Tammi. May I quote you?"

MR. LARRY AND THE DRIVER GOT OUT OF the vehicle. Mr. Larry was wide and boxy-shaped, built like a veteran wrestler going to seed. His bullet-shaped skull was ringed with a fringe of close-cropped white hair. His skin was leathery. He wore a duck-billed baseball cap, sunglasses, tan safari jacket, and baggy canvas pants tucked into the tops of a pair of old hiking boots.

The female driver was eighteen, slim, with a cover-girl face, well scrubbed and sculpted. Under her hat, her reddish-brown hair was pinned up at her nape. She had green eyes and golden skin. She wore a red kerchief around her neck, a light blue button-down blouse, tight faded jeans, and boots.

Mr. Larry crossed to Deputy Winters and Sheriff Dell, halting a few feet away from them. The driver stood on his right, a few paces to the side.

There was no handshaking between Mr. Larry and the sheriff, no exchange of pleasantries. That was a rarity in these parts, where folks prided themselves on their friendliness.

"Where is he?" Mr. Larry, his voice rough, gravelly.

The sheriff wouldn't budge. "This is a restricted area, Hummel." He was about the only person in the county to call the other by his last name, rather than "Mr. Larry."

"You're not going to throw the rule book at me when I've got a man dead, are you, Sheriff?"

"I don't want any more casualties today, Hummel. Driving on the shoulder going the wrong way is dangerous."

"Nothing dangerous about it, not with the driver I've got." Mr. Larry nodded toward her. "My niece, Debra Gale. Best driver I've ever had."

"Miss Gale and I have met before," Dell said. "In traffic court, where she was found guilty of a number of speeding violations."

"Nice to see *you* again, too, Sheriff," Debra Gale said, all cool, dry, and velvet-voiced. "Though not under the present circumstances, of course."

"I thought your driving privileges had been suspended, Miss Gale."

"They were, but they were just reinstated."

"You won't keep them long, driving like that."

"Don't blame the girl," Mr. Larry said. "I told her to do it. The way your boys have got the traffic screwed up, it was the only way to get up here. So, if you're looking to pin the blame on someone, pin it on me."

"We'll get back to that later, Hummel. For now, it's just as well that you're here. I want to talk to you."

"Talk later. Garland now. Where is he?"

"This way," the sheriff said.

The foursome moved off to the edge of the ditch. Sheriff Dell studied Mr. Larry and his niece as they eyed the burned-out wreck. Mr. Larry didn't give away much. He was the original Great Stone Face. Debra Gale's face was a blank mask, as well, but a beautiful one.

"Where's the body?" Mr. Larry said.

"In the wreck," Dell said.

"I don't see it."

"It was badly burned."

Mr. Larry grunted. "So?"

"You tell me."

"I think it stinks, Sheriff."

"I'm listening."

"Garland wouldn't drive into a train."

"According to the evidence, that's exactly what he did do."

Mr. Larry shook his head. "You ever hear of anybody broadsiding a moving train, Sheriff?"

"It happens, especially with drunks. Deke Garland's been arrested a couple of times for driving while intoxicated."

"There's not enough booze in the whole world for him to have gotten that drunk."

The sheriff shrugged. "Autopsy'll determine if he was drinking or not. Until then, let it pass.

"Sometimes an idiot driver will try to beat the train to the crossing and not make it, but that's not the case here. We know he was stopped at the crossing. Then he crashed through the gate into the train." The sheriff paused, thinking.

"What could cause that? Mechanical failure, maybe? Something slipped in the transmission, say, throwing it into drive?"

"No way," Mr. Larry said. "My mechanic had that pickup tuned like a Swiss watch."

"I don't buy it either, but I can't afford to overlook the possibility. But if you rule out Garland being drunk and doing it to himself, and you rule out mechanical failure, what have you got left?"

"Somebody did it to him."

"Foul play, you mean?"

"If that's what you want to call it."

"What do you call it? Murder?"

"I don't call it anything at all."

"But that's what you meant, Hummel. Somebody did him in. That's interesting. Why would you think that?"

"That's how it adds up. If he didn't do it—and he didn't—it was done to him."

"Deke Garland have any enemies?" the sheriff asked.

"I don't know. Maybe. Probably. He was a mean drunk, a chiseler, and a deadbeat."

"Nice fellows you've got working for you, Hummel."

"In my line of work I need tough men, not choirboys."

"What line would that be?"

"Ranching." Mr. Larry thrust his chin out belligerently. "I'm a rancher, see? That's what it says on my tax return under 'occupation'—rancher.

"If you think you've got something on me, Sheriff, file charges. Only you better be able to prove them in court."

"When I do, I will."

"Nobody has yet."

"Let's get back to Garland. Did anybody hate him enough to kill him?"

"Not that I ever heard of."

"What about you, Hummel? How did you feel about him?"

Mr. Larry shrugged. "He was a hired man, no more, no less. He did his job, as long as you kept an eye on him. I didn't have any complaints."

"Did you quarrel with him recently? Have an argument, a fight?"

"I don't know, I may have. I tee off plenty, when I catch somebody doing something stupid."

"Did you tee off on Deke Garland?"

"I may have, I don't remember. I can't remember every time I give one of the hands a cussing-out."

"Did you catch him doing something stupid?"

Mr. Larry smiled. "I know what you're doing. You're trying to make out like I had something to do with Garland's death."

"Like I said, I've got to consider all the possibilities."

"Frankly he wasn't worth killing. If I said boo, he'd've been scared out of his skin. Besides, I've got an alibi for the time of Garland's death."

"We'll check it."

"Go ahead. It's a waste of the taxpayers' money, but that's never stopped you before, Sheriff. When you get tired of that you can try looking for the real killer."

Mr. Larry turned, starting back toward his vehicle. "I've seen enough." Debra Gale followed, with the lawmen trailing a few paces behind.

Mr. Larry halted beside the vehicle, on the passenger side. "You want Garland's killer and I want

him, too. That kind of makes it like you're working for me. Funny, huh, Sheriff?"

"I'm glad you've got a sense of humor," Dell said. "Maybe this'll give you a laugh. Maybe you were the target, not Garland."

Mr. Larry scowled. "How do you figure?"

"That was a pretty flashy pickup. Everybody knows it belonged to you. And there's some folks around that don't like you too well."

"Sure, I've got enemies. What successful businessman doesn't?"

"Sure. Maybe somebody had something planned for you. Something fatal. They saw the pickup and thought it was you, only Garland got it instead."

"Not bad. That's good thinking, Sheriff. I feel real good now, knowing you're on the case."

"Could be an inside job, by someone who's close to you. Who benefits if you die?"

"Nobody," Mr. Larry said, "because I'm not going to die. I'm going to live forever.

"Don't think you can use this as an excuse to go prying around at my ranch," he warned. "I'll clean my own house, Sheriff. You find the killer."

Debra Gale said, "With a suspicious mind like that, no wonder you're a lawman."

"The top lawman in this county, Miss Gale," Deputy Winters said.

"Not after the next election," Mr. Larry said. "The only reason you got in last time was because I underestimated you, Dell. You slipped in when I wasn't looking. I didn't think the voters were dumb enough to fall for your 'good government' line but I was wrong. I won't make that mistake again."

"We'll see," the Sheriff said. "In the meantime I'm

going to do what the voters elected me to do, and that's enforce the laws."

He called to the young deputy, who was standing by the patrol cars. The deputy came over in a hurry. His name was Hallam.

"Do you have your ticket book with you, Hallam?"

"Why . . . yes, sir, Sheriff. Certainly. I always have it with me. That's regulations."

Hallam hauled out his ticket book. The sheriff pointed at Debra Gale. "Write her a summons for driving on the wrong side of the road."

"Yes sir." Hallam strode over to one side with Debra Gale and began filling out the summons.

Mr. Larry said, "What're you picking on the kid for?"

"She's getting off easy. I could have also charged her for crossing a police line and a few other moving violations," the sheriff said.

He glanced at Hallam. The young deputy was gazing adoringly at Debra Gale, dazzled by her beauty. The ticket book lay in his hand, forgotten.

"Hallam!" Sheriff Dell had to call the deputy's name a couple of times to get his attention and break the spell. Falling all over himself, Hallam excused himself from Debra Gale and trotted over to his chief.

He sighed. "Isn't she wonderful, Sheriff?"

"Stop acting like a lovesick pup and remember you're a deputy, Hallam!"

"Don't be too hard on the boy," Mr. Larry said. "She generally has that effect on men."

"I know how to handle that," Dell said. He told Hallam to get Deputy Martinez. In quick time, Hallam returned with the other.

Deputy Martinez. Isabel Martinez, a woman.

"You write the ticket," Dell told her. She was immune to Debra Gale's charms and the ticket got written. Mr. Larry sat in the passenger seat, waiting for this foolishness to end so he could get on with his life.

Winters and Dell stood off to one side, watching, talking quietly.

"Mr. Larry," Winters muttered, shaking his head. "The top crime boss in the county, and all we can hang on him is a traffic ticket. And not even on him, but his niece!"

"He's the king bee," the sheriff said.

WITHIN HALF AN HOUR AFTER SCHOOL HAD
let out on Wednesday afternoon, the student parking lot was empty of all but one vehicle, a battered
old gray sedan. The hood was open. It was an
American-made car with a six-cylinder engine.
Standing around the front of the car, peering at the
engine, were Arch Mokely and J. W. Burns. It was
Arch Mokely's car.

On the car roof sat an open toolbox. Mokely took
a tool from it and made an adjustment. He said,
"Give it a go, J.W."

Burns got behind the wheel and turned the key
in the ignition. The motor growled but refused to
turn over. He tried a few more times, with no success. He got out of the car and stood beside Mokely,
studying the engine. Mokely scratched his head.

On the east side of the building's south wing was
a paved parking lot, reserved for teachers and faculty members. Across from it was a field with a
paved basketball court. North of the court was a

dusty square of gravel-covered ground. That was the student parking lot.

While Mokely and Burns were studying the motor, two figures marched into view, rounding the northeast corner of the building. One was a long-faced gray-haired man in dark green work clothes. That was Hugo, the school custodian.

The other was Vice-Principal Bennett Brock.

Brock and Hugo walked alongside the building, moving from north to south. They paused frequently, looking up, studying windowsills, eaves, and roof gutters. Brock did most of the talking, with Hugo nodding from time to time. Once, he pointed at the juncture of the roof gutter with a corner drainpipe.

They continued on their rounds, following the edge of the building.

"What's Brocky up to with Hugo, Arch?"

"Looks like they're making some kind of an inspection tour, J.W."

"Brock must've heard us, he's looking this way. Uh-oh, here he comes."

"So what? We're not doing anything."

"He's a mighty picky fellow."

Brock angled toward the lot, leaving Hugo beside the building. He moved briskly, like a power walker, arms and legs churning. He followed a course as straight as a train coming down the tracks. He crossed the grassy area into the lot, kicking up dust.

He stopped short a few feet from the car, glaring through the thick lenses of his black glasses. His gaze took in the car, the toolbox, and Mokely and Burns.

"Hi, Mr. Brock," Mokely said.

"Mr. Brock," Burns said, nodding.

They were polite, soft-spoken, respectful. Anything less was asking to get cut off at the knees by Mr. Brock.

"What're you doing?" Brock asked.

"Working on my car, Mr. Brock," Mokely said.

"I'm helping him," Burns added.

Veins stood out on both sides of Brock's forehead. "This is a parking lot, not a garage. The student parking lot is a privilege. Don't abuse it. If you want to work on your car, do it at home, not on school property."

"It won't start. I'm trying to get it started," Mokely said. "Soon as I get it started, we'll be out of here, Mr. Brock. Gone."

"Gone," Burns echoed.

"See that you are. Otherwise, it'll be towed," Brock said.

"Yessir."

"I mean it, Mokely."

"I know."

"I've had my troubles with you two in the past. Graduation is only a few months away. Keep your noses clean."

"Yes, sir," they chorused.

Brock started to turn away, thought of something, and turned back. "You, Burns. Miss Quigley in the office tells me you haven't paid your class dues yet."

"Uh, yes, sir, that's right. I haven't paid them yet."

"It's not right. It's wrong, dead wrong. If you don't pay your class dues, you can't go to the prom,

or go on the senior trip, or attend graduation ceremonies. *If* you graduate."

"I will," Burns said. "Unless you know something I don't know, Mr. Brock."

"I know that you're a foul ball, and so's your partner Mokely here." Brock rubbed his chin, thoughtful. "Say . . . you two were in the same class as Martens today."

They nodded. Brock said, "What do you know about that insect attack? I'll tell you: nothing. You know nothing about it. Don't go talking it up. Keep your traps shut. I'm not going to let a lot of loose-lipped scare-mongering ruin our Founders' Day celebration."

"Yes, sir," Mokely said.

"We'll keep our noses shut," said Burns.

"And our mouths clean."

"You can count on us."

"We've got school spirit."

"You'd better," Brock said threateningly. "Now, get that heap out of here."

He turned on his heel, starting toward the school. He thrust forward, arms and legs working.

Not slackening the pace, he called back over his shoulder, "And pay those dues, Burns!"

He rejoined Hugo, and the two continued making their circuit. They rounded the southeast corner of the building, moving out of sight.

About ten minutes later Hugo emerged from a utility door near the middle of the east wall. He held a device that looked like a tire pump. At one end was a nozzle. Under it was a container about the size and shape of a coffee can.

He moved south along the wall, occasionally

pausing to squirt some fluid from the sprayer into nooks and crannies.

At the far end of the building, two short flights of stone stairs connected the teachers' parking lot with street level. Down these stairs came Stephanie and Rita.

They started across the lot, toward the student lot. Rita noticed Hugo spraying. She paused to watch. Stephanie halted, impatient. "Rita . . ."

"Just a second, I want to talk to Hugo."

"*Hugo?* Are you nuts?"

Rita approached the custodian. Even from ten feet away, the reek of insecticide was heavy, a thick chemical smell. Hugo spritzed some liquid into a crack in the wall.

She said, "What're you doing, Hugo?"

"What does it look like I'm doing? I'm spraying for bugs. And bees, and all other pesky little critters that fly and creep and sting."

He kept at his work, not bothering to look up as he talked. Mainly he was talking to himself.

"You just sprayed an anthill, Hugo."

"Spray 'em all! That's what Mr. Brock said. Get 'em all, don't let one of 'em get away."

Some fumes caught in Rita's lungs and she choked, coughing. Her eyes started to burn. She stepped back, into clear air, where the symptoms subsided.

She cleared her throat. "Shouldn't you be wearing a mask or something? That's pretty strong stuff."

"It doesn't bother me."

"I hope it works better on the bugs."

"It does."

About eight feet above the ground, under the bottom of an overhanging stone windowsill, was a spiderweb. In it was a spider, poised on eight hair-fine legs. Hugo lifted the sprayer and squirted a blast of fluid at point-blank range, drenching the spider and leaving a wet, chemical-smelling stain on the wall. The spider curled up into a ball, motionless.

"It works," Hugo said.

"Why'd you do that? It wasn't doing any harm," Rita said.

"Orders. Kill 'em all, that's what Mr. Brock says. He's got the wind up over that kid who got all stung up today."

"Find any bees yet?"

"Nope. No beehives, wasps' nests, or hornets. I couldn't find any. Neither could Mr. Brock, but he's got me out here anyway," Hugo said, adding quickly, "Not that I'm complaining, mind you.

"I don't blame him for being worried. Not if it's killer bees.

"What do *you* think it is, Hugo?"

He opened his mouth to speak, glancing up. He saw something that made him keep quiet. He closed his mouth, his gaze sullen, brooding.

"I've got a lot of work to do," he said, moving away, busying himself at another stretch of wall.

Rita looked up. Standing behind the window, looking down at her, scowling, was Bennett Brock.

Rita turned, crossing toward the dirt lot, where Stephanie stood by the gray car, talking to Mokely and Burns. She didn't look back, but she could feel the vice-principal's eyes boring holes into her back. Her shoulder muscles were all tensed up. They didn't relax until she reached the dirt lot.

If Brock tried to call her back now, she could always keep going and say she hadn't heard him. Or maybe not. Brock could yell loud.

Her shoulders tensed again.

She joined the others around the front of the car. "Hey, y'all."

"Hi," Mokely said. "Stephanie was saying that you two need a ride."

"Sure could. I had to go back inside before, to get my books, and we missed the bus."

"We'll give you a ride," Mokely offered.

"You got one?" Burns said, surprised.

"That's funny, J.W." Mokely saw Rita looking at the disabled motor beneath the open hood.

"No problem," he said. "I'll have it fixed pronto. Then we'll give you a ride home."

"Great! Thanks," Rita said.

Mokely leaned over the engine, screwdriver in hand. "The frammis valve needs adjusting, that's my guess. I'll just tighten this screw and open the valve. . . ."

He worked on the engine. Stephanie said, "What'd Hugo have to say?"

"Not much, after he caught Brocky giving him the evil eye," Rita said.

"He gave *us* the evil eye. Me and Arch," Burns said.

"He sure did," Mokely said, over his shoulder.

"And he sure can give it."

"He sure can." Mokely straightened up, taking a step back, screwdriver in hand. "Give it a go, J.W. No, never mind, I'll do it myself."

"I can do it."

"No, I'll do it. It takes a special touch. I know this car," Mokely said.

He got behind the wheel, one foot resting on the ground. He turned the key. After a few false starts, the engine fired up, coming to life with a vroom.

Burns closed the hood, then he, Stephanie, and Rita got in the car. Mokely was grinning. Success! He gave the thumbs-up.

He put it into drive. It rolled forward a few feet, shuddered, and stalled. When he tried to start it again, the engine wouldn't catch.

"You've got a special touch, all right," Burns said.

"I know what's wrong. I'll have it fixed in a minute," Mokely said, grinning. He went back to work under the hood.

Five minutes later the grin was showing strain around the edges, but it relaxed when the engine turned over and hummed along with no signs of stalling.

Arch drove out of the lot, onto a paved roadway that ran past the teachers' parking lot before curving around in a ninety-degree angle that put it on a straight course due east toward a cross street.

Ahead, Hugo trudged across the road, angling toward a utility shed at the corner of the field. The gray car slowed to let him pass, then rolled up alongside him.

Mokely stuck his head out the open window. "Watch out for killer bees, Hugo."

"Let 'em come. I've got my trusty spray gun." Hugo waved the piece of apparatus.

"Why don't you use some on Brock— Who said that?" Mokely looked around in the car, as if trying to spot the speaker. "Why, J.W. Burns, I'm ashamed of you, saying such a thing about our beloved vice-principal!"

"I didn't say it, you did."

"Nice try, J.W., but it won't work. Next you'll be trying to put the blame on Rita or Stephanie."

Hugo said, "Never mind with all your smart talk about Mr. Brock. Trying to get me in trouble or something!"

He walked off, grumbling. Mokely eased his foot down on the gas. The car hesitated, almost stalling, then lurched back into the groove.

Mokely let out his breath. The car rolled east on a blacktop road, under an arch formed by the boughs of trees lining both sides of the road.

Mokely shook his head. "It's been one strange day."

"Weird," Burns said.

"Bee-zarre," said Stephanie. Rita looked at her.

"Now you've got me doing it," Stephanie said.

THE CAR WAS RED WITH A BLACK INTERIOR. IT was a sharp, fast muscle car, capable of doing a hundred and twenty miles per hour on a straight-away. At the present time it was doing about a half mile per hour. That was its average "speed."

At this very moment, however, exactly 4:30 P.M. on Wednesday afternoon, it was doing zero miles per hour. It was sitting still, stuck in traffic. Behind the wheel sat Albert.

It wasn't easy to find a traffic jam out in these wide-open spaces, but this was a special occasion. It wasn't every day that a train smeared a car in a fatal crash. A lot of workers at the plant had left when their shift ended at four o'clock, adding their numbers to the long line of cars stretching along the highway's southbound lane. Everyone wanted to see the crash site, though there wasn't much that was visible from the road. Adding to the mess were the vehicles unable to use the now-blocked crossing, forcing them to take an alternate route.

There was some traffic on the highway's northbound lane, going into town. Not as much as that on the southbound side, but some. The highway was a major truck route and a fair amount of big-rig truck traffic was always passing along both sides of the road, night and day. Now there was enough northbound traffic to prevent those in the opposite lane from beating the jam by driving down the wrong side of the road. Which didn't stop some characters from trying it anyway, only adding to the chaos.

Such a one was Albert. When he'd gotten into the lane, it was still moving. When he topped a low ridge and saw the jam laid out below him, it was too late to turn back. Behind was a long line of cars, bumper-to-bumper. Deputies were keeping the opposite lane clear so official vehicles from town could reach the crash site. Anyone who tried to switch lanes was immediately ticketed and sent to the back of the line.

Albert was locked into the line, his red car a link in a chain of vehicles that dragged across the landscape with painful slowness.

The engine rumbled, shaking the car. Even while idling, the big motor used up a lot of gas. He couldn't use the air conditioner while the car was just sitting there, or it would overheat. Steam hissed from the radiators of some cars along the line that had already overheated. They sat on the side of the road, hoods open, venting steam clouds.

Albert had all the windows rolled down, but the inside of the car still felt like an oven. He played the music on his tape deck loud. People in cars ahead of him turned around to locate the source of the noise. The people in the car behind him put

their hands over their ears. Albert played his pop
tunes until a deputy told him to cut it out.

The crossroads was the heart of the jam. The
west branch, out to the railroad crossing, was
closed off. Some traffic was being diverted to the
east branch, which led after a mile or two to a
lesser road running parallel to the highway.

The red car neared the intersection. Albert
planned to turn left, onto the eastbound road. A
big-rig truck in the northbound lane had the same
idea. It was a big semi-tractor trailer, too big for
that tight turn. It might have made it if the trailer
had been hinged in the middle.

The trucker jockeyed the rig, angling it back and
forth across the intersection square. What with all
the other vehicles, there wasn't much room to
move. Making the turn would be a lengthy process.

A couple of deputies were standing in the square,
trying to direct traffic. Ahead of Albert, a couple of
cars had moved up, leaving an open space. Behind
him, horns honked.

A deputy came over and said, "Move that car."

"I want to make a turn," Albert said.

"I don't care what you want to do. There's a couple of patrol cars trying to get through and they
can't because you're blocking the road. So move it."

"But—"

"Get that car out of here or I'll pull it off the road
and have it impounded!"

"All right, I'm going!"

"Watch your tone, boy," the deputy said, glaring.

The red car pushed forward, past the turn. Two
cars managed to slip in behind it before the deputy
could stop them. He stopped the third car in line,

leaving the space clear so the patrol cars could enter the westbound cross street.

After they passed, the southbound traffic crept forward, closing the gap. Albert was boxed in. Ahead, the line of cars stretched to the top of the next ridge, and beyond.

"Big man," Albert said, sneering at the deputy, whose back was turned to him, and who was out of earshot. Even so, Albert said the words under his breath.

The line inched forward. Motion flickered on his right, in the field sloping up toward the railroad embankment. A vehicle drove downhill, trailing a line of dust. It had left the dirt road and angled downward across the open field. It didn't need a road, dirt or otherwise, to go where it pleased.

It came to him, a safari Range Rover that rolled to a halt, pulling up alongside the red car, about ten feet away.

Up close, you could see that the line of dust trailing it was really a cloud. It drifted through the open windows. Albert couldn't see through it. He started coughing.

After a moment the dust settled, revealing passengers in the Range Rover—Debra Gale and Mr. Larry. Mr. Larry leaned forward, around the driver, a hand cupped to his mouth.

"Albert! I could spot that fancy red car of yours a mile off," he said. From his tone, he sounded like he didn't have much use for showy cars.

Albert said nothing. With Mr. Larry, that was often for the best. When he wanted to hear from you, he'd tell you what to say. Albert looked

straight at Mr. Larry, careful to avoid any reckless eyeballing of the delectable Miss Debra Gale.

"Come out to the ranch tonight, Albert. I've got a job for you."

"Who, me, Mr. Larry?"

"I don't see any other Alberts around. And that's a blessing, I might add. Anyway, you're always asking for a chance to show your stuff, so here it is."

"Great."

Mr. Larry scowled. "You don't sound too happy about it."

"No! No, I'm happy, Mr. Larry. I'm just surprised, that's all."

"You look it, with your mouth hanging open like that."

Albert realized his mouth was hanging open and closed it.

"That's better," Mr. Larry said. "You looked like a hicktown rube getting his first look at a carnival midway.

"Come to the ranch after dark," Mr. Larry continued. "It's an all-nighter, so don't figure on getting home before morning. Tell your mother so she won't worry." From his tone, he sounded like he didn't have much use for mothers, either.

"I wouldn't use you at all, but Garland's death left me shorthanded," Mr. Larry said, jerking a thumb back in the direction of the crash site.

"Deke Garland? That's who got killed?"

"Your mouth's hanging open again."

Albert shut it.

"I don't want to see that no more, Albert. It's nasty."

"Sorry, Mr. Larry. I knew about the crash, but Garland . . . ! What happened?"

"He broadsided a moving train. Wrecked a perfectly good pickup truck, dang him."

A voice shouted, "Hey, you!" It came from the red-faced deputy, the one who had told Albert to move on. He came hurrying over, approaching the red car on the driver's side.

He was sweatier and more red-faced than ever. He wanted to get to the Range Rover, but the cars were lined up bumper to bumper, with no room to get between them.

He leaned across the red car's hood, neck muscles cording as he bawled at the Range Rover's occupants. "Hey, you can't drive over there!"

"No? We're doing it," Mr. Larry said, eyeing him coldly. "Let's go Debra."

"See you, Albert," Debra said, winking. She put the vehicle in gear. The wheels spun, throwing up dust clouds.

"Hey!" the deputy shouted, dodging along the line of cars, waving his arms. "Stop, stop!"

Then the dust clouds engulfed him and he seemed to vanish from sight.

Albert sat in his car, coughing. It was like being in a plane and flying through a cloud, only this cloud was made of fine reddish-brown dust that settled on the seat cushions and dashboard. All he could see was dust. It got into his nose, making him sneeze.

The dust settled, thinning. Shapes took form in the murk, gradually returning to solidity.

The Range Rover arrowed south across the field, already a distant blur and shrinking fast.

The red-faced deputy ran back to his car, but before he even got there, the Range Rover was out of sight.

Albert said to himself, "Debra Gale! Wow!"

He had a lot of time to think about her because the line still wasn't moving.

IN THE NORTHEAST CORNER OF THE TOWN WAS a section called Hillandale, a quiet neighborhood of modest single-family houses. That's where Rita lived. Her parents were both employed at the Syntrex ChemWorks. Her father was an industrial engineer, and her mother was a supervisor in the administrative department.

Now, on Wednesday evening, Rita was driving home with dessert. She sat behind the wheel of her mother's car, a no-frills compact model, basic but efficient.

Seated beside her was her twelve-year-old sister, Audrey. She was waiflike, with a brown ponytail and big brown eyes.

There was another sibling, a brother, but he was away at college up north.

The Knight sisters were coming back from a Kwikee convenience store, a few blocks away from where they lived. Ordinarily they would have walked, but it was near dinnertime, so they took the car. In the back, on the floor, was a Kwikee bag filled with a half gallon of ice cream and some other items their mother had asked them to get.

The windows were rolled down. Rita didn't bother with the air conditioner. By the time it started working, they'd be home. Besides, the sun was going down, making things cooler. In the west, the sky was orange.

Rita stopped for a red light. From behind the backseat, a bee rose into view, buzzing. It floated into the front, hovering between Rita and Audrey.

Audrey made a face, reaching to bat it away.

"Sit still," Rita said. She was motionless. The bee bounced around under the ceiling, zigzagged a few times in front of her face, and drifted out the window.

Rita rolled up the window. The bee flew back, bumping against the glass. The rear window was open. No power windows here. Each had to be rolled up by hand.

The bee started rearward, toward the open window. Rita looked both ways. The road was clear. Before the bee could fly in, she stepped on the gas and drove away.

"You drove through a red light!" Audrey squealed.

"Yeah, well, it's better than getting stung," Rita said.

"I don't believe it, you drove through a red light!"

"Audrey . . ." Rita said warningly.

"It's a good thing for you no cops saw you! If Mom and Dad found out—"

"They won't. Will they, little sister?"

"What'll you give me for not telling?"

"What'll I give you if you do."

"I won't tell."

"That's a good girl."

Audrey sank back in the seat, shaking her head. "I can't believe you ran a red light. That's pretty cool."

"It's stupid, but I couldn't think of anything else—what are you staring at?"

"You should see yourself, Rita! You're white as a ghost! Are you okay?"

Rita nodded. Audrey said, "You don't look okay. I'm sorry, Rita, I was just teasing. I wouldn't tell on you, you know that.

"I didn't know you were scared of bees."

"I wasn't," Rita said, "until today. Let me tell you what happened to Ox Martens. . . ."

ALBERT HUNG AROUND THE APARTMENT UNTIL
about nine P.M. that Wednesday night. He sat in
the living room watching TV with his mother, a
small, slight, prematurely aged woman.

The apartment occupied the ground floor of a
three-story wood-frame building in the southwest
quarter of town. The neighborhood was respectable,
though shabby and fading. The same could be said of
his mother. She'd had a hard life. She'd dropped out
of high school at sixteen to get married. She had to.
Her husband had died before Albert reached his
first birthday, shot dead outside of a pool hall. Albert had no memories of him. His mother had never
married again, raising Albert by herself. She didn't
drive, so she'd stayed here in town, where she could
walk or take a bus to her job as a waitress in a
downtown café. She was Mr. Larry's cousin. He'd
helped her out with small interest-free loans once
or twice, during especially hard times.

She'd raised Albert the best she could, but even

she had to admit that, outside the home, he could be "quite a handful."

The apartment was dim, except for the TV set, a window opening on a rainbow-bright world.

Albert's mother said, "This is nice, son. I can't remember the last time you stayed home at night so we could watch some TV and visit."

"Yeah, it's been nice," Albert said. He rose from the couch, stretching. "But I've got to get going, Ma."

"So soon?"

"Can't keep Mr. Larry waiting."

"No, you can't do that," she agreed. "Just what is it exactly that you're going to be doing, dear?"

"Donkey work. Lifting and toting and hauling. With Garland dead, they're shorthanded out at the ranch. They need another strong back to help out so they don't fall behind schedule."

"I suppose."

"Hey, Ma, he's doing me a favor. There's a hundred guys that'd jump at the chance if I don't. Besides, we can use the money."

She sighed. "If you're working all night, what about school tomorrow?"

"I'll be done before then."

"You can't go to school after staying up working all night."

"So, I'll stay home and get some sleep."

"And miss school?"

"One day isn't going to matter, Ma. Anyway, it's not like I have a choice. Mr. Larry's been good to us and I can't let him down. I don't want to get on his bad side."

She fell silent, accepting the inevitable. But she didn't like it. She was fretting.

"Gotta go, Ma." He bent down, leaning forward to kiss her on the forehead. She patted his cheek. He straightened up.

"Be sure to give Mr. Larry my regards."

"I will, Ma."

"Find out when the funeral's going to be."

"Probably not for a couple of days yet. But I'll find out."

His mother shook her head. "What do you suppose could have gotten into Deke Garland to make him do such a thing?"

"Booze, probably."

"Albert!" she said sharply, scandalized. "You shouldn't speak ill of the dead."

"The guy crashed into the side of a train. He must've been drunk or crazy, and Garland wasn't crazy."

"Well, never mind. He's gone to meet his Maker, and it's not for you or I to pass judgment on him."

"Gotta go, Ma."

She gathered herself to rise out of her chair, gripping its arms with clawlike hands. He said, "Don't get up. You've been on your feet all day, so you might as well give them a rest."

She sank back gratefully, a small birdlike woman with sad eyes. "Thanks, I *am* a bit tired."

"No wonder, as hard as you work. That bad leg giving you much trouble?"

"No, not much," she said brightly. He'd seen her limping before, so he knew she was lying, but he didn't let on.

He said, "Can I get you anything while I'm up?"

"No, thanks, I'm fine."

"I'll lock the door on my way out."

"When you get home, I'll make you some breakfast."

"I might not be back before you leave for work. Sometimes these jobs run a few hours late. So don't wait for me. And don't worry."

"Albert . . ."

"Yes, Ma?"

"Be careful."

"I'm always careful, Ma."

He went into the kitchen, grabbed his hat, and said so long. He left by the back door, locking it. He rattled the knob to make sure it was locked. There'd been a lot of break-ins and burglaries in the neighborhood lately.

It was a warm night. The garbage cans at the back of the building were full to overflowing. They stank. Albert wrinkled his nose, breathing shallowly to minimize the smell.

The backyard was mostly bare dirt and weeds. A couple of cars were parked there, Albert's and the other tenants'. A driveway ran along one side of the building, opening on the street. The yard was enclosed on three sides by a chest-high wire fence. The other buildings on the street had similar layouts. Most of the structures had sagging rooflines. The neighborhood was old long before the Chem-Works had come to town, and the subsequent boom had passed it by.

A few yards away dogs barked. In the distance more barking could be heard. A lot of people in the neighborhood kept dogs, penning them outdoors at night. They could spend hours yapping back and

forth at each other. The dogs, that is. Occasionally the neighbors, too.

There was the sound of air conditioners laboring away. Through other open windows came snatches of TV soundtracks, music, voices. From a block or two away came the sound of breaking glass, like a bottle being busted. A bottle of booze, in this neighborhood. An empty, no doubt.

That set the dogs off in a new round of howling.

Albert stepped down from the back door, crossing to his car. It was parked on the side, away from the others. He took good care of it. For years he'd worked hundreds, if not thousands, of hours at crummy part-time jobs to earn the money for it.

He leaned over the driver's-side door, keys in hand. Something whined past his ear, buzzing.

Albert jumped—but it was only a mosquito, silhouetted for an instant against the yellow rectangle of a shaded window at the back of the building.

He swatted at it, missed. "I'll kill you," he said, but it flitted into the shadows, out of view.

He got into the car. Before he could close the door, the mosquito flew inside, clearly visible under the ceiling light. It landed on the side of his neck and he slapped it, smearing it across his fingers.

"Gotcha!" Albert said.

He started the car, easing it down the driveway. As it nosed into the street he could see the Chem-Works in the distance, rising above the tops of a row of tenements like an emerald city.

14

OSBOURNE WAS A BIG TOWN WITH SMALL-town ways. Most citizens were in their homes for the night by eight P.M. on weeknights. By eleven, they were in bed with the lights out. At midnight the center of town was like a ghost town.

But the plant never slept. The Syntrex Chem-Works was in operation twenty-four hours a day, seven days a week. It would have been inefficient and costly not to keep going around the clock. The big jobs were done during day shifts, when the work force was at full capacity. The other two shifts had far smaller crews, carrying out less complicated but still important tasks.

At night, the plant chugged along like a steam engine at half power. Chemicals were sorted, mixed, and processed. In the great vats and tanks they were boiled, distilled, and re-formed. The compounds were pressurized, squirted through mazes of tubing, and put through a series of chemical "baths," adding or subtracting ingredients as

needed. Finished products were sealed in storage tanks, and new processes begun.

The plant hummed along like a beehive.

Most of the processes were automated, controlled by machines, but a certain number of crew personnel were needed to watch the machines.

It was a well-designed system with plenty of built-in fail-safe devices. Automatic mechanisms recognized and aborted dangerous situations before they occurred. If the pressure in a tank neared the red line, auto-valves would open, dropping the pressure back into the safety zone. It was all done automatically, with computerized monitors and sensor banks and remote-controlled machinery.

In other words, it was idiot-proofed against major catastrophes, even if the human operators fell asleep at the switch.

Scattered at key places throughout the complex were control rooms, where technicians sat at computerized consoles, monitoring the ongoing processes in their section.

One of Syntrex's most important products was "Sucralex" an artificial sweetener much in demand by the makers of diet soft drinks, lo-cal desserts, and the like. The plant pumped it out by the railroad-tanker-carful.

At about 1:30 A.M. on Thursday morning, the Works had just finished cooking up a batch of Sucralex. The pressure in the tank was equal to that in the depths of the sea. It could have crushed a human being into a pulpy mass the size of a tomato-paste can.

The cooking process was complete. Now the pressure had to be lowered. Auto-remote mechanisms opened safety valves at the top of a tank as tall as an office building.

It vented a thick green cloud that smelled like bananas.

A light wind was blowing from the north at a speed of a few miles per hour. It nudged the green cloud, pushing it south. The air was calm and the winds were mild, so the cloud pretty much held its shape as it drifted south.

15

THE MOON WAS GREEN. IT HUNG HIGH OVER-
head, shining down on a lonely nightscape. It was
open country, out in the middle of nowhere. There
were no lights, no structures, no fences. The only
sign of human life was the vehicle crawling south
across stony fields.

The vehicle was running dark, except for its
parking lights. They were yellow-brown disks on
the front of the machine, like the glowing orbs of
some hard-shelled beetle.

It was a utility truck, a rugged vehicle not unlike
those used by phone and power companies to make
field repairs. Behind the cab, the truck bed was enclosed by a boxy metal van. It was like a camper
van, but without windows.

Albert was driving. Beside him sat Reb Ralston,
one of Mr. Larry's hands.

The truck jounced forward at a speed of about
eight miles per hour. It was a rough ride over hard
ground, but the machine had four-wheel-drive and
a heavy-duty undercarriage and shock absorbers.

The parking lights shed a ghostly golden glow, enough to pick out rocks, potholes, and other obstacles on the route ahead. Moonlight helped, too.

In the cab, Ralston said, "Tired, kid?"

"No," Albert said.

"Then how come you're yawning?"

"How come I had to be at the ranch at ten o'clock, when we didn't leave until three-thirty?"

"Because Mr. Larry said so. And like everything he does, there's a reason for it. Drive out early in the night, when there's other cars on the road, you blend in with them. Nobody gives you a second look. Drive out later, after midnight, say, and you stick out like a sore thumb. Lawman sees you, he says to himself, 'Wonder where that fellow's going this late at night? Think I'll follow him along, make sure he's not up to no good.' Savvy, Albert?"

"I get it. Pretty smart."

"You bet. Mr. Larry's got things all figured out. Sorry to keep you up past your bedtime, but this is the best time to be doing what we're about. You should've grabbed yourself a couple of hours shuteye back at the bunkhouse."

"I wasn't tired."

Ralston nudged him in the ribs. "Can't sleep for thinking about Debra Gale, huh, Albert?"

"She's all right."

"She's given lots of fellows sleepless nights."

"You included, Reb?"

"Not me. She's a money gal with expensive tastes. You got to have big bucks to go out with her, and frankly, my bank account just don't measure up.

"I saw you mooning after her like a lovesick calf, though."

Ralston's tone was cool, mocking. Albert didn't like to be needled, but he kept quiet. Ralston was a dangerous man. He was in his late twenties, built like a heavyweight fighter, except that in the bunkhouse and jailhouse brawls he'd taken part in, there was no referee to keep you from getting your head beat in or your spine stomped flat.

He was thick-featured, with arched bushy eyebrows, thin slitted eyes, and a two-day growth of beard stubble. A scar in the corner of his upper lip bared a tooth, giving him a wolfish look.

He had a long criminal record and had served time for manslaughter. The guy he'd murdered was another no-good and had been trying to kill Ralston at the time, so Ralston only spent a few years behind bars.

A bad man to mess with. Albert was a little scared of him. So, like a lot of others, he took Ralston's ribbing and kept his true feelings to himself.

"What time is it, Reb?"

"About a quarter to four."

"You think they'll be there?"

"They'll be there. Wild horses couldn't keep them away. They've already done the hard part, sneaking across the border without getting caught. They're not going to miss the gravy train. And that's us."

Albert steered to avoid a tombstone-sized rock. "I wouldn't think there's much money in smuggling illegal aliens across the border."

"It adds up. Besides, we don't smuggle them across the border. They smuggle themselves across the border. Once they're in the clear, they go to the meeting place and all we do is pick them up and drop them off.

"It's a basic dollars-and-cents proposition. People love to scream about stopping illegal aliens from coming into this country. That's what they say publicly. Privately, they know we couldn't get along without them.

"If the farmers and ranchers hereabouts had to pay their hands a decent living wage, they'd go out of business. Most of them are only a few short steps from going bust already. If they had to pay legal wages, they couldn't afford to get a crop planted, tended, or picked.

"Now, for the illegals, what they get paid here is a fortune compared to what they could get back home in Mexico, assuming there was work to be gotten. Which there ain't, generally speaking.

"It's a good deal all around. The illegals get the work, the farmers stay in business, and everybody else looks the other way. Except for some pesky lawmen and immigration agents, which is where Mr. Larry comes in.

"He's a middleman, see, a kind of contractor. He gets the illegals to the farmers, and they pay him a fee for delivering the bodies."

"And we're the delivery boys," Albert said.

"Right. Ordinarily, Garland would be doing the driving, if he hadn't tried to dispute the right of way with a freight train. So we needed a new driver at short notice, somebody who knew what he was doing and could be trusted to keep his mouth shut. We couldn't find anybody like that, so we chose you."

"Ha-ha."

"Just kidding, Albert. So far, you're not doing too bad."

"I grew up around here. I know these back trails by heart."

At that moment the truck lurched into a dip, bottoming out against the ground, bouncing the riders around in the cab. Albert clung with both hands to the steering wheel. Ralston hit his head against the ceiling, the blow cushioned by his cowboy hat.

"Dang you, Albert, you made me crush my hat!"

"Sorry."

The top of Ralston's hat was crumpled. He took it off and put a fist in the crown, punching it into shape before putting it back on his head.

He felt around his pockets, then relaxed. "Lucky you didn't break my bottle, boy, or you'd be in deep doo-doo."

He pulled out a pint bottle. In it, liquid sloshed. He uncapped it and took a long swallow. The reek of strong whiskey fumes filled the cab.

"Ah. I'd give you a taste, Albert, but you're driving."

Ahead, about a hundred yards away, rose a low ridge, topped by a line of trees. Above it hung the moon, swimming in a hazy sky. The moon was the same shape and color as a breath mint.

"Green moon," Albert said.

"Green Mist. The plant unloaded a cloud of its crud tonight. I saw it drift past the ranch an hour ago," said Ralston.

"I can smell it."

There was a smell of bananas.

"Slow down," Ralston said. "The meeting place is on the other side of those trees, at Bender's Ford."

Albert halved the speed, dropping it down to about three miles per hour. Ralston opened the glove compartment. Inside was a tiny globe light, which came on when the lid was lowered.

He reached in and pulled out a gun, a big-caliber automatic pistol. He checked the clip and chambered a round, easing down the hammer.

"What's that for?" Albert asked, straining to keep his voice level.

"Insurance," Ralston said. "These illegals are generally peaceful enough, but you never know when there's going to be a few wolves among the sheep. You could live pretty good off of what you could sell this truck for on the other side of the border. This gun is in case anybody gets some big ideas."

Light from the instrument panel and the glove compartment underlit his face, making his features appear thicker, more menacing. The scar on his mouth made him look like a grinning devil.

"Don't worry, Albert. I haven't had to shoot anybody for a long time."

"Who's worried? How about a gun for me? I can shoot."

"You just drive. I'll take care of the rest."

"How many people are we picking up?"

Ralston shrugged. "I don't know—eight, ten. . . ."

"How're you going to fit them all in the van box?"

"Are you kidding? You can fit fifteen guys back there."

"Six is more like it."

"I said they could fit, Albert. I didn't say nothing about them being comfortable. Once we had twenty-two in there. They wasn't all adults, though. There was a couple of kids. One of them died from the heat, and two adults. Mr. Larry sure raised cain about losing those adults!

"You can't make money off a dead man," Ralston concluded.

"No, but Mr. Larry's probably working on it," said Albert.

The rise neared. Up close, gaps appeared in what had seemed to be a solid wall of trees. There was a sound of running water.

Albert pointed the truck at one of the gaps. Ralston grunted. "You know the way, huh, kid?"

"I've fished Bender's Ford plenty of times."

"This time we're fishing for men."

The truck crested the top of the shallow ridge and rolled into the gap. The trail wound through a patch of woods, trees pressing on both sides. Branches arched overhead, making the trail resemble a tunnel through the brush.

The dark path was striped by moonbeams slanting through the trees. Albert got a whiff of the musky smell of plants and soil. Above all, he could smell bananas.

Green Mist always falls eventually to earth like rain. Sometimes it fell within a few hundred yards of the ChemWorks, other times it fell miles away, depending on the speed and direction of the wind, the humidity, and other local weather conditions.

Ralston made a face. "That sweet smell is turning my stomach."

"It *is* strong," Albert agreed. "The mist must've just come down."

"It don't set too well with the booze, I'll tell you that."

There was light at the edge of the tunnel. Moonlight, touched with the faintest tinge of pale green. The truck broke into a clearing.

"Stop," Ralston said. "We're here."

THE CLEARING WAS PART OF A GRASSY BLUFF.
It was about twenty-five yards across, from the
edge of the woods to the far end. It was the flat top
of a riverbank. The bank sloped down to the
riverbed, about twelve feet below. The rivulet was
one of the branches of the Chochoya River, the
main watercourse in the county.

The river here was about twenty feet wide and
shallow, no more than three feet deep at its center.
This was Bender's Ford, named for an old-time out-
law and rustler who used to run stolen horses and
cattle on both sides of the border. Since his time,
the crossing had served as a favored thoroughfare
for vast numbers of fugitives, bootleggers, gunrunners, smugglers, and illegal aliens. The border was
so wide, and the Border Patrol personnel stretched
so thin, that the crossing rarely if ever came under
watch by the authorities. When it did, the big-time
border jumpers somehow managed to find out
about it, so the raids netted nothing but a handful
of small fry.

"Keep the engine running," Ralston told Albert. He got out of the truck cab. The ceiling light was switched off, so no light flashed when the door was opened.

Ralston tucked the pistol into the top of his belt. He picked up a long-handled flashlight. The lens was taped to permit only a sliver of light to shine.

Albert stuck his head out the window, peering into the darkness. They were alone on the bluff. The overhang at the far edge of the bank blocked his view of the water straight ahead. On the sides, to the left and right, the bank curved away, so he could see parts of the river upstream and downstream. Smooth boulders studded the riverbed, rising above the water. The river flowed slow, flat, and smooth, except for frothy trimmings around the rocks.

The water made gurgling, chuckling sounds. There was another sound, too, more felt than heard, a vibration. Albert could barely make it out over the throb of the idling engine.

"I don't see anybody," he said, speaking low.

"They're here," Ralston said. "They're just hiding until they're sure we're not immigration men."

He worked the flashlight, turning it on and off in a simple series of signals. The narrow beam from the hooded lens was too thin to dazzle their eyes, by now accustomed to the darkness.

"That's the recognition signal," Ralston said, repeating the pattern three times.

Nothing happened. Ralston swore and tried again, with another three reps.

"Nothing, huh?" Albert said, after a long pause.

"They're around, somewhere. They've got to be."
Ralston ran the signal three more times.

"Hear that, Reb?"

"What?"

"A hum."

"I don't hear it."

"Like a high-tension line, or something."

"None of those around here, kid. It's the river."

Albert wasn't so sure, but the harder he listened, the less sure he was of what he heard. Maybe it was the river, at that.

He said, "Are we early?"

"No," Reb said. "They should've been here hours ago."

"Maybe they got lost."

Ralston shrugged. "Maybe. You stay here. I'm going to take a look around."

"Think there might be trouble?"

Ralston bared his teeth, in what was more of a snarl than a grin. He patted the butt end of the pistol sticking out of the top of his pants. "They ain't made the trouble that this can't handle, kid."

He started forward. He hadn't gone more than a few paces when Albert called, "Watch out for snakes."

Ralston gave him a dirty look and kept on going. He shone the thin-beamed flashlight on the ground ahead. The likelihood of a black moccasin snake or a rattler being found so near the water was far from remote. The thin line of light proceeded slowly over the ground, picking out a path.

Ralston moved through weeds and clumps of grass, stirring up the grains of Green Mist that had recently fallen. The banana smell thickened, filling his nose.

He walked forward, toward the bank. Beyond the woods the bluff was clear, bare of trees, boulders, or other cover. Except for a few scraggly knee-high bushes and the ankle-high grass, there was no cover, nothing behind which even a single person could hide.

In the east, the darkness was lifting, becoming charcoal gray. Ralston raised the flashlight beam from the ground, shining it into space. It shone across the river, a thin horizontal strip of light showing against the trees topping the opposite bank.

Even when he was within a few paces of the edge, the overhang kept him from seeing the riverbed directly below. He heard something. He halted, listening. He'd thought it was part of the rush of the river, but it wasn't. Now that he was closer, he could make out two sounds—the river rush . . . and something else.

The something else was a deep humming drone, like the lowest note on a bass fiddle. There was something almost mechanical about it, but not quite. Not so much mechanical as *bio*mechanical.

It sounded like a snoring giant. Giant *what*? Something inhuman. No, nonhuman. There was something familiar about it, nagging at the frontier of recognition. He'd heard it before, or something like it. . . .

The gun was in his hand. He picked his way to the edge, looking down. Now he could see the river. The side of the bank was a steep dirt slope. At its

base, about ten feet below, was a flat stretch of shore, covered with smooth flat rounded stones. Cattails and rushes grew thickly at the water's edge.

Then Ralston saw it. Sprawled along the shore in the postures of violent death were a half dozen or more bodies. Human bodies, the corpses of the illegals he was supposed to meet.

There's a name for criminals who prey on illegal aliens crossing the border: *coyoteros*. At first, for an instant, Ralston thought it was *coyoteros* who had gotten the migrants. They were capable of acts of incredible violence and thought nothing of taking human life. Ralston cursed himself for showing himself in the open with the flashlight in his hand, where he made a big fat target for any lurking gunmen.

But before his startled brain could unfreeze and switch gears, he realized that here was strangeness far beyond the doings of any mass murderers.

The moon shone straight down into the riverbed, lighting the scene with the stark clarity of a high-quality black-and-white photograph. Or, rather, black-and-silver. The moonlight was silver, with the faintest tint of green. River rocks stood out like clean-picked skulls. Ripples and even bubbling froth showed on the water's surface.

Nearer, on shore, the bodies were covered with shadows. The shadows were multilayered. There were mounds of them, heaped high. And they were moving. They were in a state of constant motion, crawling over the corpses, revealing glimpses of twisted bodies and contorted limbs.

The shadows rustled. Moonlight glinted on what looked like scales. The mounds were made up of hundreds, thousands of tiny scaled objects. And they hummed. The mounds hummed with activity. They were the source of the low moaning drone.

No *coyoteros* here. But what was it? The hooded flashlight didn't give off enough light to see the totality of the harrowing scene, its narrow beam picking out only tantalizing, mystifying glimpses of the mound-stuff.

Ralston moved along the edge, angling for a better view. As he did so something touched his foot. He froze, looking down.

A body lay facedown at his feet. It had been over at the side, out of the light, and he hadn't noticed it until he'd almost stumbled over it.

It was one of the illegals. Whatever had killed the others by the water, this one had managed to survive long enough to scramble up the bank and throw himself over the top before collapsing. His arms were stretched out in front of him. Ralston's foot had brushed against the dead man's hand.

He shone the light on the body. The narrow beam picked up what looked like a jeweled gauntlet, as if the dead man were encased in a magnificent suit of golden scaled armor.

Ralston had to *see*. He tore the tape off the lens, unmasking a blazing beam of light. Before he focused it on the body, the buzzing started, and he knew what had caused this slaughter.

From head to toe, the body was covered with bees. Each bee made up a link, a unit, of what looked like a suit of glittering scaled armor.

The bodies on shore were similarly covered, buried under mounds of living bees. There must have been fifty thousand, a hundred thousand, or more.

Up they flew.

*B*ZZZZZZZZZZZZZZZ!

When he heard the buzz, Albert *knew*. The windows were rolled up without his even thinking about it. He just did it.

Buzzing? That really didn't describe it. It sounded like a chainsaw symphony.

Across the clearing he could see Ralston, outlined at the edge. His back to the truck, he crouched, flashlight in hand. The unmasked beam was a crystal ray, bright, pure, and powerful.

The mass of bees came boiling up off the corpse at Ralston's feet, exploding into a cloud. Their buzzing rose in pitch, getting higher, angrier. But theirs was just a small part of the deep-throated hum rising from the far greater numbers massed below at the riverside.

In a matter of seconds the first batch of bees was on Ralston, savaging him. They were a whirring, whirling mini-tornado, a buzz saw. They were all over him, on his hands, his face, nose, mouth, eyes.

The flashlight beam slashed crazily across the scene as Ralston flailed at the bees, trying to beat them away. He dropped the flashlight. It went out.

Darkness. Nothing but the sounds of buzzing and Ralston's screams. His screams sounded like an old-time car horn, going *ah-oogah, ah-oogah.*

Then there were shots, loud slamming blasts from Ralston's big-bore gun. Each shot was accompanied by a muzzle flare, a spear blade of yellow-and-red flame leaping from the gun barrel, lighting the scene like a flashbulb. They came in quick succession, one after the other, flickering like a strobe light. Each blast was a snapshot of Ralston's dark figure staggering under the assault.

He emptied a clip into the air. No more than a handful of bees were wiped out by his wild shots. And there were thousands more, many thousands.

The bullets ran out, the hammer clicking on an empty chamber. No more shots meant no more muzzle flares, and the scene returned to darkness. The blasts had drowned out Ralston's screams, but now they could be heard again.

The parking lights shed a golden globe of light that reached only a few yards beyond the truck. Beyond that was blackness, a furious chaos of sound, and whirling motion.

Albert had to see what was happening. He switched on the headlights. The sudden glare was dazzling, blinding him for a few seconds.

Squinting, he peered through the brightness. At first, he didn't see Ralston. That was because the older man had stumbled away from the clearing, toward the side. His figure was crude, bulky, ape-like. That's because it was covered with so many bees.

Behind him, the backdrop looked like a hailstorm in reverse. Instead of hailing from sky to earth, it was hailing from earth to sky. Each piece of "hail" was a bee, hurling itself from the riverside into the air. Thousands of bees, tens of thousands, rising into a cloud that dwarfed the batch now swarming Ralston.

The bee cloud towered thirty feet high, seething with marbled streaks and swirls, marking bands of greater or lesser concentration. They streamed and flowed in the blaze of the headlights.

An arm peeled off the cloud, a tentacle six feet wide at the base, narrowing to a fine questing point. It wiggled around in the air above Ralston, as if feeling around for him. The tip of the point halted, turned downward, and arrowed toward him, raining hundreds of more bees down on his head.

He dropped to his hands and knees. Albert had seen enough. He switched off the lights, afraid that they would bring the bees down on him.

The scene went black. Albert sat rigid, paralyzed with fear, swimming in cold sweat.

What'll I do what'll I do what'll I do—

He couldn't hear Ralston screaming anymore. The buzzing grew louder, like the ripping grinding roar of a garbage-disposal unit, infinitely magnified.

They're getting closer, he thought. They've finished off Ralston and now they're coming for me. But they can't get me. I'm safe in here. . . .

Was he? He had to make sure that the cab was airtight, that there was no entryway, no matter how small, that they could use to get at him.

He started to move his arms but couldn't. He was gripping the steering wheel with both hands. He hated to let go because the wheel was something real, something solid, unlike the nightmare world that was now engulfing him.

He unpeeled his hands from the wheel and turned on the ceiling dome light. Suddenly three phantoms sprang into being around him, ragged ghosts with haunted eyes and shouting mouths.

Albert was shouting, too. He realized that the ghosts were images of himself, reflected on the side windows and windshield. When he stopped yelling and shut his mouth, they did the same.

Things started hitting the truck. Bees. It was like a rainstorm. First, there were just a few bees, like the first few fat drops of rain pattering on the glass, in advance of the storm. Albert flinched as each one hit.

Then there were more, and they were coming faster. A steady drizzle of bees touching down on the cab, crawling around on it. The pace increased until they were coming so fast that Albert couldn't flinch enough to keep up. He went into a prolonged shudder.

His eyes rolled, trying to look everywhere at once. The windows were closed tight. He turned around, squirming in his seat to see the back panel of the cab. There was a peephole opening on the van box, the size and shape of a brick. It was covered with a steel plate that could be slid open. It was closed now. Albert ran his fingertips over it, making sure it was secure.

The truck was old, rusty. The cab looked intact, but if the body had rusted away anywhere to make even a dime-sized hole, he was in big trouble.

"I'm already in big trouble. If there's a hole, I'm dead," he said. He had to speak loud to hear himself over the buzzing. It felt like it was rattling the plates of his skull.

"Keep cool keep cool," he said. It was hard to talk, because he was having trouble catching his breath. But it was worth the effort to hear something besides the buzzing.

"Keep cool and don't do anything stupid," he told himself. "Gotta get out of here. *Carefully.* I'm safe inside. They can't get me unless I do something stupid."

He reached to start the car, freezing his hand on the ignition key. It was already in the on position. The engine was idling, as it had been all along, since his arrival at the clearing.

He'd forgotten about it. That's what fear could do, blank out the mind and paralyze the will.

"It'll take more than that to scare me!" he shouted, half sobbing.

"More than that" was not long in coming. Something slammed into the front of the truck with a tremendous blow. Albert cried out. He couldn't see what it was, not with the overhead light turning the windshield into a mirror.

He switched off the light. Pink-and-yellow afterimages floated before his eyes in the few seconds of darkness before he switched on the headlights.

He groaned. The number of bees was greater than ever, falling on the truck. There were so many

that it was dismaying. It was a rain of bees, a whirlwind of bees.

But they hadn't made that banging jolt that rocked the truck. That had been done by something big and solid. Whatever it was, Albert couldn't see it. It was hard to see through the massing bee cloud.

Something hammered the front of the truck. Albert jumped. He craned, trying to see what was doing the hammering, but it was below eye level, out of sight.

That was when a pawlike hand reached up, fastening on the hood. It was shaggy, pulsing with motion. It was covered with bees, layers of them, interlocking, crawling back and forth all over each other, wings fluttering, tails raised with stingers at the ready, seeking a swatch of flesh to skewer.

There was precious little to be found, since nearly every square inch of skin was swarming with stinging bees.

A second hand appeared, fastening onto the hood with a thump. It, too, was layered with living bees.

Albert sat frozen, staring as the owner of the hands pulled himself up into view.

It was a shaggy man, a crude apelike figure that seemed made of bees. Somewhere inside the creature was Reb Ralston. He should have been dead, but the raw animal vitality of the man was keeping him going. Somehow he had managed to crawl to the truck.

Time stood still. Albert trembled in a seeming eternity of terror, but in reality only a handful of seconds had gone by since the swarm first attacked.

Ralston opened his mouth. It, too, was lined with

bees. Leaning against the truck, he began feeling his way around the front fender, toward the driver's side.

He banged against the vehicle, giving it a pounding. He couldn't see, not with his eye sockets jammed with squirming bees.

Some idiot was babbling nonstop, shouting with fear. Albert realized that it was he himself, but he couldn't stop.

Out of the headlights, the bee-man was a shadowy ragged horror, looming up the other side of the driver's-side door. He felt around for the door handle, pawing it.

He was trying to get into the truck. The door wasn't locked. Albert locked it.

The bee-man managed to lock clumsy fingers around the handle and pull, but it wouldn't open. He beat bee-mittened fists against the door and window, smearing bees against the glass. He was weak and his blows didn't have much strength in them, and they were growing weaker with each heartbeat.

He slipped to his knees, dropping down below the window. All Albert could see were his hands scrabbling at the glass. Then they unclenched, fingers opening, and sank from sight.

As if responding to a signal, the bee cloud broke on the truck with full force. Shadows filled the cab as insects crowded the windshield and windows, blocking the light. They were all over the cab, flowing over it like water.

Bees covered the glass, massing. Albert felt like he was being walled in. Walled in by bees. Their segmented bodies in the hundreds rustled against

the truck. The windshield was covered with them. Their armored bodies were interlocking, like pieces of a mosaic. A living mosaic.

He couldn't see out the windshield. He couldn't see where he was going.

He switched on the windshield wipers. They swept broad areas clean, brushing off layers of bees. Other bees were squashed by the wiper blades.

"Ha-ha! How do you like that, suckers!" Albert hissed. He spoke low, afraid that the bees would hear him and become even madder.

A line of squashed bees began to build up outside the arcs of the wipers. The sweeping motion enraged the bees, who kept swarming the blades, becoming paste under their movements. They kept coming, and the blades left broad viscous smears on the glass that made it hard to see through.

Albert put the truck in gear. The trail was behind him. He couldn't drive through it in reverse. He had to turn around and go through it headfirst.

He drove forward, into the clearing, to get enough space to make a U-turn. The bees swarming the cab shrilled, sending the humming into a higher pitch, one that seemed to set the metal vibrating.

The wipers squeaked and squealed. The windshield was plastered with yellow-brown paste. Albert could barely see. He remembered the windshield auto-cleaner and hit it, sending twin jets of cleaning fluid spurting on the glass.

That helped, for a few seconds. Then more bees threw themselves under the wiper blades, once more fouling the glass.

Driving nearly blind, Albert wrestled the wheel,

turning the truck around. He thought he was in the clear, until a thin sapling tree went under his right rear fender.

But he was turned around, facing the trail mouth. It was hard to spot it. He leaned over the wheel, squinting through the clouded glass.

Ahead lay what looked like a solid wall of trees. He hit the cleaning fluid again. This time the spurts were less forceful; there was obviously less fluid.

One section of the trees looked darker than the others. The trail? He pointed the truck toward it, inching forward. The bee cloud hung over the truck, engulfing it. The darkness crackled with seething, furious motion.

He heard a thump as the front wheels ran over something: Ralston. Another thump followed shortly as the rear wheels passed over him.

That was good. It meant that Albert was on the right way toward the trail. He kept steering toward that patch of deeper darkness.

Tree branches beat the roof and sides of the cab, splintering, breaking. The truck lurched into the tunnel through the brush.

He couldn't see through the smeared windshield. The wipers were laboring. He had them on top speed, but they were slogging through a few jerky, shuddering strokes. The paste of crushed insects was so thick that it was slowing them down almost to a halt.

The truck rolled onward. Albert wanted to get as far as he could while he was still able to see at all. The truck was doing ten, fifteen miles an hour. The

bumps of the trail were tossing him around in the cab, his rear end rising clear off the seat.

He couldn't see! He was driving completely blind. A low branch smacked the windshield so hard that Albert feared it was broken. Before he could step on the brake, he heard a crash.

The truck stopped dead. But Albert kept moving. His head hit the windshield with a crunch.

18

"**A**TTENTION, STUDENTS. THIS IS VICE-PRINCIPAL *Brock speaking. Today, Thursday morning, after attendance is taken in homeroom, all students will proceed to the auditorium, to hear the speeches of the two finalists competing for the honor of representing Sibley High School during this year's Founders' Day celebration. After the speeches, students will return to their homerooms to cast their ballots. Votes will be tallied and the winner announced this afternoon.*

"That is all. This is Mr. Brock, signing off."

Blat! went the intercom in every room in the school at the conclusion of Brock's message, when the PA system was switched off.

The auditorium filled up with the nine hundred or so members of the student body, plus faculty. The space rang with loud talk and the sound of bodies moving around in seats. At the back of the hall, the doors were closed. A couple of teachers stood watch, making sure that nobody tried to sneak out.

At the opposite end of the hall was a proscenium-arched stage. The curtains were closed. Beyond them protruded the stage apron, which was about ten feet wide. The boards had an amber waxy look, like a gym floor.

At both ends of the stage apron, short flights of steps connected to the auditorium floor. On stage, to the audience's right, stood a speaker's podium with an attached microphone on a gooseneck stand.

Rita was seated with the rest of her homeroom classmates to the right of the central aisle, about a third of the way back from the stage. She spotted Stephanie sitting with her homeroom, a few rows away. They caught each other's eye and Rita gave her a little wave. Stephanie waved back.

The two finalists, of course, were Tammi and Jean. Tammi wore a sleeveless red blouse and a blue skirt. Jean wore a thin one-piece dress and a single strand of pearls.

Tally, sitting beside Rita, said, "Check it out, Jean's dress is in the school colors."

"That's a nice touch," Rita said.

"Think those pearls are real?"

"Probably. She's got rich folks."

"Wish I did. Who're you going to vote for, Rita?"

"I'm going to listen to both speeches and give them a fair hearing before I vote for Jean."

"Yuck. I can't stand her. She's so perfect."

"I know what you mean, but at least she's not Tammi."

Tally nodded. "There *is* that."

"And then there's her chum, Lucy. There's another good reason not to vote for Tammi, not that I need it."

"How do you like her blouse? If it was any tighter, Tammi'd be outside of it."

"That should win her some votes from the boys."

"They're such dogs."

"For sure," Rita said. "Speaking of dogs, where's Albert? He didn't come to school today."

"I heard some of Ox's jock friends are blaming Albert for Ox getting stung," said Sally.

"That wouldn't keep Albert away. He's not afraid of them. He's a weasel, but when he gets in a fight, he's a holy terror."

"Like a cornered rat."

"But not as likable," Rita said.

Jean and Tammi both had their campaign managers in tow. They were on opposite sides of the auditorium—Jean and Caro on the left, Tammi and Lucy on the right. They moved down the aisles toward the stage, chatting and politicking with various seated students along the way.

Tammi and Lucy passed the row where Rita was sitting. Tammi sneered at her; Lucy looked through her. Rita blew them a kiss. A few rows ahead, Stephanie saw them coming and made a face.

Jean and Caro sat down in the first row on the left side of the center aisle, Tammi and Lucy sat on the right.

The lights dimmed, filling the hall with rich golden-brown shadows. Overhead lights shone down on the stage apron.

Bennett Brock bounded up the stage stairs, taking his place behind the podium. The students quieted down. Teachers shushed those who hadn't been struck dumb by the mere sight of the vice-principal.

Brock tapped a finger against the microphone, testing it. It sounded like corn popping, electronically amplified. He adjusted the mike, leaning into it. He started to speak, only to be silenced by a loud feedback squeal. He put a hand on the microphone, covering it, and glared offstage, into the wings, where a couple of tekkies from the student stage crew were frantically trying to fix the sound. Finally, they got it right.

Brock spoke into the mike. "Before we begin, I have a message for the student body from Principal Twonky. He asked me to read it to you."

Tally whispered, "Why doesn't he read it for himself?"

"Mr. Twonky never comes out of his office," Rita whispered back.

"What's he look like? I don't think I've ever seen him."

"Me, neither. I don't know anybody who has," Rita said. "Maybe there *is* no Mr. Twonky."

"I wish there was no Brock," Tally said.

Mrs. Hanford, their homeroom teacher, heard them talking and snapped her fingers at them, signaling for silence.

Brock unfolded a sheet of paper and held it under the tiny speaker's light on the podium.

He read the message, quoting the principal as saying that Founders' Day belonged to a great tradition, and a great part of that tradition was the election of a student to the crown of Queen Javelina, to represent Sibley High School in the town's official holiday celebration. He expressed his confidence that, no matter who the winner was, she would be a credit to her school, her town, and the great state of Texas.

"That lets out Tammi and Jean," Tally observed.

"Shush!" Mrs. Hanford said.

After finishing the principal's message, Brock added a few remarks of his own, closing ominously with: "Don't let me catch anybody giving less than one hundred and ten percent school spirit!"

With that, he left the stage, to a smattering of halfhearted applause. What clapping there was came from those who were glad to see him go.

The president of the student council stepped up behind the podium to say his bit. He was greeted with less applause than Brock. He was a high-school senior, but his speech contained as many windy generalities as that of a veteran politician.

He explained the format of the program. Each candidate would be introduced by her campaign manager and then make a short speech. The candidates had tossed a coin to see who would go first. The winner was Jean, who chose to have the last word. So, Tammi would go first.

There were some rude noises from the audience, so the student council president, whose name was Ken Fennel, cut short his remarks. Brock circled the aisles, glaring, peering, but he couldn't catch the noisemakers.

Ken Fennel announced Tammi's name. Tammi and Lucy rose, to dutiful applause. They climbed the stairs at the right side facing the stage, crossing the apron in front of the curtains toward the podium on the other side. There was some whistling and yee-haws from the boys when they caught sight of Tammi in her tight blouse.

"Knock it off!" barked Brock. The offenders knocked it off.

Ken Fennel moved away from the podium, making room for Lucy and Tammi. Lucy rushed the microphone and would have elbowed him out of the way if he hadn't moved. He stepped into the wings.

Lucy was bouncy, full of pep. Her eyes shone and there were red spots of color in her cheeks. She could hardly stand still. She was short, so she had to adjust the microphone, pulling it way down low. It was still too tall for her. She folded her arms across her chest and started tapping her foot. She looked around, irked. Tammi came up on one side and Ken Fennel came up on the other, but they didn't know what to do, either.

There was a ripple in the audience and some nervous laughter. Lucy's face was red, her expression fierce.

Out from behind the curtains came Ernie Anderson, one of the stage crew. He was a pencil-necked geek with a Woody Woodpecker haircut and thick black glasses held taped together at the nose by a Band-Aid. When he showed, there were some appreciative chuckles from the audience, and a few low mooing calls of, "Ernie, Ernie!"

He raised a hand, bobbing his head in an aw-shucks manner. One of the same voices that'd been calling his name said, "Yo, nerd!"

There were some snickers. Ernie blushed, his face falling. He went to the podium to do his job. Lucy, Tammi, and Ken Fennel moved aside. At the base of the podium was a folding stairstep. Ernie bent to pull it out, bumping his head on the microphone, causing a loud *bop!*

That got some laughs. When they died down, a voice called, "Dweeb." Flustered, Ernie wrung his hands.

Near the podium, in front-row seats, were Jean and Caro. They exchanged glances, Jean smiling behind her hand. She was too much the politician to be seen openly enjoying her rival's discomfort. Not so Caro, who grinned hugely.

Ernie pulled out the footstep. It was designed for situations like this, when the speaker was too short to reach the microphone.

As Ernie rose, stepping back, a white object came sailing out of the audience, not too far from the stage. It was an egg. It went over the heads of those at the podium, hitting the wall behind them, near the stage arch. It cracked, spattering. Some of it landed on Ken Fennel's clothes. Most of it was a runny yellow smear on the wall.

There was a loud collective gasp, like in a courtroom when a witness drops some bombshell testimony. Rows of heads turned, looking for the egg thrower. The egg thrower, too, took part in the charade, turning in his seat, frowning, making a show.

But it was no good: he had been seen by the viceprincipal. Brock charged down the center aisle, a little dynamo. He ducked left into a row and went down it sideways, moving crablike past seated students. In the middle of the row sat Chubb Wynant, a meaty wiseguy with wavy brown hair and a face as round as a pie pan. A line of pimples circled his smirking mouth.

He stopped smirking when Brock grabbed him by the collar and hauled him out of the seat. Chubb was whisked to the end of the row and into the aisle. Brock hustled him toward the rear of the auditorium, Chubb's feet barely seeming to touch the floor. They exited into the hall, the door swinging shut behind them.

Lucy was so mad, she looked like she was going to burst a blood vessel. Her face was red, her eyes bulged, and her neck was corded. She gripped the side of the podium, white-knuckled.

Tammi slipped past her, speaking into the microphone: "Nice try, Jean." She smiled when she said it, to show it was a joke. It got a laugh and broke the tension.

Jean, smiling frozen-faced, gave Caro a sharp sidelong glance.

"She's just guessing," Caro said, out of the side of her mouth so only Jean could hear it. "She doesn't know anything and she can't prove anything."

"Unless Chubb talks," Jean said, behind her hand.

"For twenty dollars, wild horses couldn't drag it out of him. And he doesn't get the money until later. If he snitches, no deal."

"That was smart, Caro."

"That's why I'm your campaign manager."

"Too bad he missed," Jean commented.

19

SOMEONE SOMEWHERE WAS BEATING A BIG
bass drum, thumping the blazes out of it: *boom
boom boom.*

The drum was Albert's head, the drumming the
sound of his pulse. He was awake. He was alive.
The way he felt, he wished he was dead.

He stirred, groaning, his eyes still unopened. His
head ached. He had the all-time worst headache.
He was hot, he felt like he was stewing. He panted
for breath. He was thirsty, parched. He felt sick to
his stomach.

He ached all over. He felt like he'd been worked
over by a baseball bat, and maybe a lead pipe or
two. He was in the truck cab, slumped behind the
wheel.

It was daylight. The windshield was fouled with
yellow-brown smears. Green things, leaves and
branches, pressed against the cab. Judging by the
amount of sunlight filtering through them, it was
about mid-morning. It was hot, very hot.

A spiderweb of cracks ran through the windshield where his head had struck it. He was lucky the glass hadn't broken, letting in the bees.

The *bees*! Where were they?

He sat up straight, sending waves of pain rattling through him. He groaned aloud, alarmed by how feeble he sounded.

He didn't see any bees around. The windshield was badly smeared, but the side windows were pretty clear. Tree branches pressed the glass, but if any bees were there, he'd have seen them. He saw only the remains of crushed, dead bees, stuck to the windows.

Maybe the others had gone away.

He was in no hurry to find out.

He felt around his face. On his forehead, near the hairline, was a big fat lump where he had hit the windshield. It was throbbing, each pulse spiking his skull with pain. The skin had split and bled, and now his face was stiff with streaks of dried blood.

He was about ten feet off the trail. He could guess what had happened. He'd hit a tree and the truck had stalled. That killed the engine, preventing it from catching fire and burning. But the lights were on, during the hours that he'd been unconscious after hitting his head. During that time they'd drained the power and now the battery was dead. So there was no starting the truck and driving out of there.

He'd have to go on foot. And soon. The sun had been beating down on the cab. Inside, it was like a greenhouse, a sweatbox. Beads of moisture condensed in the corners of the windows.

The air wasn't too good, either. It was thick, choking. Albert reached for the window handle, to roll it down and let in some fresh air. Then he thought of the bees and froze, hand on the handle. After a while he let go, wiping his sweaty palm on his pant leg.

Were the bees gone?

If not, all he'd have to do is lower the window, opening it a half inch, and that would be the end of him.

He checked himself for injuries. His chest and ribs were sore, from hitting the steering wheel, but nothing was broken. He could walk if he had to. If the bees would let him.

There didn't seem to be any around, as far as he could tell. Of course, his viewpoint was limited. Were the bees gone? he wondered again. If so, how far had they gone? Far enough for him to get away?

By pressing his face against the window on the passenger side and squinting through the spaces of leafy tree branches, he could determine his location.

The truck was close to the end of the trail, about thirty feet away. It had veered off to the left, plowing through ten feet or so of brush before hitting the tree. The trail twisted, so its mouth was diagonally across from the passenger-side door.

At trail's end, he noticed a hole in the trees, opening on a patch of gray-brown meadows and a glimpse of sky. A half mile or more of open ground lay between the truck and the highway.

He would have to abandon the truck and trek out to the highway. From there he could catch a ride to Mr. Larry's ranch. A lot of truck traffic moved along

the highway and truckers were generally big-hearted characters, ever ready to lend a helping hand. At least that's how they were portrayed in the songs.

He'd hate to be caught in the open by the bees—while crossing the fields, say, or even waiting by the roadside trying to hitch a ride. . . .

He couldn't see the highway, but he thought he could hear it, a rumble of distant traffic. Or was that the bees? Maybe it was just the sound of the blood thudding in his ears with every heartbeat.

What of the bees? *Had they flown on ahead, into town?*

He hoped so, because that would mean that they were gone from here, giving him a chance to escape alive.

He remembered how Ralston had looked, at the end. The bee-man. Even the inside of his mouth had been lined with bees. . . .

That memory was a powerful incentive for Albert to stay put.

AFTER THE EGG-THROWING, THE REST OF THE program proceeded without incident. Lucy made a one-minute speech introducing Tammi. Tammi made a five-minute speech demonstrating why she should be voted Javelina Queen. Somehow it was all tied up with what she described as her hope for world peace. . . .

Caro followed, winding up her sixty-second intro by saying, "Don't get stung! Vote for the best candidate. Jean's got the buzz!"

That won her some points, since everybody knew that Brock frowned on any kind of bee talk, no matter how frivolous. But at that moment the vice-principal was absent from the auditorium. He was in his office with Chubb Wynant, raking him over the coals.

"You're suspended as of right now," Brock said. "No, cancel that. You'd enjoy not having to come to school. Well, mister, by the time you get out of detention for this little caper, you'll be old enough to qualify for Social Security.

"Do you know what Principal Twonky said? He said that you had committed an *un-Texan act*. That's what he said. By heaven, Wynant, you'll pay for this.

"And you'll pay the cleaning costs for Ken Fennel's clothes, too."

Meanwhile the assembly drew to a close, and everyone returned to their homerooms. En route, Rita overheard two girls talking.

"That Tammi is such a little tramp, with her too-tight blouses," said one. The other nodded.

"Did you see that Chubb Wynant? What an idiot!"

"And he can't even throw straight."

"I'm sorry Lucy didn't get it. I'd love to see her with egg on her perky puss."

"Ditto."

Back in homeroom, Mrs. Hanford handed out the ballots. A blank box had been drawn beside Jean's and Tammi's name in which to mark one's choice. Rita voted for Jean, because she was not Tammi. She folded her ballot, which Mrs. Hanford collected along with the others.

THE CHOCHOYA RIVER RAN THROUGH OS-
bourne. It was the presence of water in this arid
land that had caused the town to spring up many
years earlier. It was necessary for livestock, com-
merce, manufacturing. The town had grown up
around it. The river was routed through the devel-
oped area by an aqueduct, a U-shaped concrete
trough set below street level, ten feet deep and
twenty-five feet wide. Both sides were topped by
eight-foot-high wire fences. It was bridged at intervals by cross-street overpasses.

South of the courthouse square, bounded on one
side by the river, a small park had been built. During the day, there were always a few people, mostly
retirees, fishing off a nearby bridge. Occasionally
the water yielded up a catfish, crawdad, or eel.

The fishermen liked to stand at the end of the
bridge, under the shade of the trees edging the
park. This morning two such anglers, both old duf-
fers in baggy, colorless outfits, were trying their
luck. One wore a battered canvas hat with a few

lures stuck in the band. The other wore a Houston Astros baseball cap.

Waist-high concrete walls, topped by tall chain-link fences, lined the sides of the bridge. At the end of the bridge, where it met the land, there was a section of wall without a fence. That's where the two fishermen stood, leaning over the top of the stone wall, dangling the lines of their fishing rods into the chuckling shadowed river below.

Neither of the duo said much. They didn't have to. Long stretches of silent time rolled by. It was good to be outside, out of the house, warming old bones. Good to be alive.

The two were ancient, looking like a pair of wrinkled old turtles who'd been stripped of their shells. Their eyes glinted with slow dim awareness, the orbs of sunning reptiles hoarding their last flickering reserves of strength.

Abruptly, the canvas-hatted oldster's line went taut, the rod bowing. Whirring sounded as the reel spun, letting out line.

"Looks like you've got a bite," the other said, with mild interest.

Canvas Hat let out plenty of line, slackening it. The line had seemed in danger of snapping, but now that he'd allowed some play in it, the threat lessened.

He started reeling it in, slowly. The rod bent almost double, forming an arch.

"Must be a whopper," said the man in the Astros cap.

"Feels like I hooked a spare tire," Canvas Hat said.

At the end of the line, where it disappeared into

the water, he noticed a disturbance. The surface rippled, uneasily. A line of bubbles floated to the top.

Something moved underwater, something big. It rose, breaking the surface. It was a corpse, a human body. It looked worse than terrible. Luckily, most of it was underwater and couldn't be seen too well. The fishhook was somewhere embedded in corpse flesh. That was a pleasant thought.

"Oh my," Canvas Hat said.

"You look like you're gonna have a stroke," the other said. "Are you?"

Canvas Hat swallowed hard. "No. I don't think so."

"Better land that, then," Astros said.

Canvas Hat steered the corpse to the side, out of the main current. It floated facedown, its shoulders and upper back above water. It was the body of a short, dark-haired man in a T-shirt and jeans.

It was one of the illegals who'd been killed by the swarm at Bender's Ford last night. A few of the victims had fallen into the river and been washed downstream. This one had negotiated the twists and turns of the watercourse, its rock and rapids, to finally be swept along into the aqueduct that ran through town.

The duo didn't know that. All they knew was that they had a dead body on their hands.

"I'll call the sheriff," said the Astros-cap man. He started toward the park. The pay phone was only a hundred yards away.

Canvas Hat stood at the side, in the shade, watching the corpse bob in an eddying backwater. While he stared, shocked, another body came float-

ing down the river. He watched it stream past, round a corner, and vanish from sight.

After a while some patrol cars rolled up, disgorging deputies. One of them stuck his head over the rail and looked down at the thing on the other end of the line.

"Holy smoke! It *is* a body," he exclaimed.

The man in the Astros cap had been picked up by one of the cars, directing them to the site. Now he strutted back and forth, hands behind his back, chest puffed out.

"Who'd you think you were dealing with, a couple of senile old coots who were seeing things?" he said.

The first deputy shook his head. "A dead body! I don't believe it."

"You should've seen the one that got away," Canvas Hat said.

MIDDAY. THE SUN WAS DIRECTLY OVERHEAD, baking down on the truck cab, turning up the heat on Albert. The cab was an oven. He was panting.

There was a bottle on the floor on the passenger side. A pint bottle, that had belonged to Ralston. A mouthful of liquid remained in it.

Albert was dry. That is, his mouth and throat were dry. The rest of him was sweat-soaked. Every breath sent moisture pouring out of his pores. He was greased with sweat. He stank. But inside, he was dry. His mouth was a dust bowl. His throat was a dry hole drilled in the desert.

Sunlight glinted on the bottle. He reached for it. The motion sent his heart hammering. His head threatened to explode. He thought he was going to pass out. His vision dimmed, but after a few heartbeats the shadow faded and he knew he wasn't going to faint, not this time.

He grabbed the bottle and sagged in the seat, breathless. When he felt better, he sat up. His hand trembled, agitating the liquid in the bottle he held.

It took almost more strength than he had to unscrew the cap. That scared him, because it meant that he was fading. The reek of raw alcohol fumes made his stomach heave. But the crystal-clear liquid looked so cool, so refreshing. . . .

He raised the bottle to his lips. The fumes made his eyes tear and turned the inside of his nose. He wet his fingertips with the stuff and rubbed them against his cracked, split lips. They tingled, burned, then felt cooler.

Steeling himself, he took a swallow. The reaction was immediate and explosive. It felt like the top of his head had been torn off. He coughed, spewing out the mouthful, each droplet a jolt of acid. If there'd been anything in his stomach, he'd've lost it.

The coughing fit didn't do anything for his aching head. Each spasm hit like a sledgehammer.

He was wet-eyed, gasping. Trust Ralston to be fueling himself with a high-octane brew. It was white lightning, clear grain alcohol, ninety percent pure spirits. Albert could've gotten the same effect by touching his tongue to a live car-battery terminal.

It looked like water, but it was liquid fire. There was nothing in it for him. Funny, very funny. In a rage, he almost hurled the bottle away from him, thinking of how satisfying it would be to bust it into a million pieces—

Uh-uh. Hold it, boy. Whoa. Mustn't do that. Might break a window and let the bees in. What bees? He hadn't seen any for hours. Which didn't mean they weren't out there, waiting for him to grow impatient and do something stupid and then they'd have him.

But that was crazy. Bees weren't hunters. They

didn't have the smarts to play a waiting game, stalking a human victim. But these were no ordinary bees, they were killer bees, and that made all the difference. Who knew how their little bug minds worked? He'd never heard of bees swarming at night, either, but they had, thousands of them. Just ask Ralston. He wouldn't be able to answer, though, not with his mouth filled with bees the way it was. Plus he was dead.

Albert had to do something. The cab wasn't entirely airtight. Enough oxygen managed to leak in through micro-fine seams to keep him alive— barely. But the air was stale and foul and hot.

He rolled down the window, opening it a razor-fine crack, just to let in a trickle of fresh air.

Was that buzzing he heard? He froze, listening. Maybe it had been the sound of a branch rustling against the glass. Or it might have been nothing at all, nothing but his imagination.

He assured himself that the slit at the top of the glass was too narrow even for a bee to pass through.

He saw no bees. Outside the cab lay the end of the trail, open fields, freedom. Fresh air and later a cool drink, a hot meal, a bath, and sleep.

All he had to do was open the door and get out. Unless the bees were around, in which case he'd wind up like Ralston.

He stayed put.

THE BALLOTS FOR SIBLEY HIGH'S QUEEN JAVELINA contest were totaled up by a three-member panel of teachers whom Bennett Brock had arm-twisted into "volunteering" their free period to counting votes.

It was a secret ballot, unsigned, so the usual quota of jokers had their fun writing in responses that weren't in the questionnaire. Among the ballots were eleven write-in votes for Chubb Wynant, who was currently occupied scrubbing egg off the auditorium stage wall.

The trio added up the numbers of legitimate votes and declared a winner. The collective voice of Sibley High School had spoken, choosing its queen. The tabulators turned over ballots and the result to Brock.

"Thank you," he said. "You're giving one hundred and ten percent school spirit and that's what's expected of all of us here at Sibley, students and teachers alike."

They had used up about a hundred percent of

their break time, so after they reported to Brock, they immediately had to go to their next classes.

Miss Quigley, the blue-haired secretary receptionist in the administration office, was scandalized by a particularly offensive ballot that the trio had singled out for attention.

In the place listing the voter's choice, somebody had written, in big block letters: MR. BROCK'S MOMMA.

Miss Quigley tsk-tsked as she passed the ballot across a desk to Brock. Brock read it, smiling grimly.

"I should think you'd be outraged, Mr. Brock."

"That's just what this hooligan wants, Miss Quigley. I wouldn't give him—or her—the satisfaction."

She nodded tightly, with birdlike head motions. "These days, the girls are as bad as the boys."

"What I get from it is the respect, Miss Quigley. Notice that this sick-minded individual, with this moronic scrawl, still calls me *Mister* Brock. Not Brock, mind you—or worse—but *Mister* Brock. Respect, Miss Quigley, respect." He stopped, as if struck by a sudden thought.

"Well, fear, actually," he added.

Soon after, the schoolwide intercom system buzzed with a bulletin:

"Attention, students. This is Vice-Principal Brock speaking. The results are in. The winner of the title of Queen Javelina of Sibley High School is Jean Collier. You have elected Jean Collier as your queen for this year's Founders' Day. On behalf of Principal Twonky and myself, congratulations to the winner,

and to the first runner-up, for showing what school spirit is all about. That is all."

"I think I'm going to throw up," Tammi said.

"That's what school spirit is all about," said Rita.

OSBOURNE COUNTY HOSPITAL, LOCATED IN town, was fairly new, modern, and efficient. In the basement, there was a morgue. It wasn't something the hospital advertised to the general public, but it was there. The part-time county medical examiner was a full-time doctor on the hospital staff. He did autopsies in cases of violent or suspicious death, or deaths for which no attending physician had issued a death certificate.

The post was one of Sheriff Dell's innovations, part of his effort to put local law enforcement on a businesslike, scientific basis. The ME's salary was paid out of sheriff's-department funds. There was a county coroner, too, whose responsibilities were the same as the ME's. The coroner job was an elective office. The coroner was paid out of county funds, but from a different department than the sheriff's. He didn't care, as long as he got paid. He didn't care if the ME did all the work, either, since it left him more time to spend on cronyism and politicking.

The ME was named Kornblatt, Dr. E. K. Kornblatt. He was small, middle-aged, his hair neatly barbered, and with a thin mustache. He wore a white lab coat over a natty suit and tie.

At the moment he was bustling around the autopsy room, circling the dissecting table. It was made of stainless steel and the slab tabletop had built-in drains. To one side, hanging from the ceiling like a drop lamp, was a medical scale for weighing organs. There was a wheeled instrument table. Laid out on sanitary white linen were rows of sharp gleaming instruments.

On the table lay a corpse, covered by a sheet. Nearby stood a wheeled gurney, on which lay another corpse, also sheet-covered. An arm hung down below the sheet. It looked like the forearm of Popeye the Sailor, of cartoon fame, but there was nothing funny about it. The forearm was grotesquely swollen, ballooning into a hand with fingers the size of candy bars. The limb was an angry purple-red color.

The autopsy room was part of the hospital's basement morgue. In the background you could hear the hum of refrigerating units, the gurgle of fluid running through tubes. Overhead were banks of cold bright fluorescent tube lights. The mingled smells of disinfectant, ammonia, alcohol, and formaldehyde served to mask the smell of death. Almost.

In the room with Kornblatt and the corpses was a hospital orderly and Sheriff Dell.

Dr. Kornblatt moved to the head of the table, near the body's head. A sheet covered the body from head to toe. Kornblatt's rubber-gloved hands gripped the edge of the sheet.

"Let's see what you called me away from my lunch for, Sheriff," he said.

He lowered the sheet, uncovering the corpse to the waist. It looked like a life-size inflatable human doll that had been blown up, overblown to just this side of bursting at the seams. A purple-red doll.

"Hmmm," Dr. Kornblatt said. "Interesting!"

The orderly crowded closer, with keen interest. He was a young-old man in his early twenties with a high forehead and thinning blond hair, very fine, like corn silk.

"There's something you don't see every day—and now, two in one day," he said, rubbing his hands.

"This guy really likes his work," Dell said.

"Never mind about him," Kornblatt said. "The cadaver was fished out of the river, you say?"

"Yes. Literally," Dell said.

Kornblatt nodded. "I can see the hook is still in him."

"He didn't die from drowning."

"You don't say," the doctor exclaimed, sarcastic.

Dell's ears burned. "What killed him, Doc?" He knew the ME hated to be called "Doc."

Kornblatt studied the corpse, holding his chin. "Hmm."

"Those wounds that are all over him. Punctures, like somebody went to work on him with an ice pick. The other one, too." Dell gestured toward the corpse on the gurney. "Could be it's a gang killing, a double homicide."

He pushed back his hat, scratching his head. Lawmen always keep their hats on, even indoors. It

must be part of their job description. "But what could make them swell up like that?"

Kornblatt glanced toward the gurney. "The other is in the same condition? . . . Yes, I can see that he is, judging by the arm."

The orderly eagerly turned down the sheet, baring part of the body. Dell said, "We found this one a couple of miles downstream."

"Any identification on them?"

"None, Doctor. And no leads. The way they look now, their own mothers wouldn't recognize them. It's not the first time bodies have turned up in the river, but it's the first I've ever seen like this. A body that's been underwater long enough will swell up—"

"No, no." Kornblatt made impatient chopping motions with his hand. "That's not it. The bodies haven't been dead long enough to produce the characteristic swelling associated with gases of decomposition.

"This swelling action is different. It is not caused by the processes of decay. These are recent corpses. At a rough guess I'll say they haven't been dead more than twelve hours, and that's allowing for the retarding effect of being immersed in water." He paused.

"This swelling is the product of an extreme allergic reaction."

"Allergic reaction?" Dell said. "Allergic to what?"

Dr. Kornblatt pressed rubber-gloved hands together, making a steeple. "Those puncture wounds were caused by stings. A great many stings, each loaded with venom. Massive dose! The swelling is a symptom of the bodies' allergic reaction to the venom. Of course, a dose that large would have brought about almost instant death."

"They were *stung* to death? What've we got here?"

Kornblatt looked him in the eye. "Bees, Sheriff. You've got bees."

MR. LARRY WAS ON THE CASE. THAT WAS one sure thing in a world gone mad, where killer bees swarmed and slew. The heavens might fall, but Mr. Larry would keep on keeping on, taking care of business.

The proof of that lay in the Jeep that came rolling up the hill toward the mouth of the woods trail to Bender's Ford. Albert heard it coming long before he saw it. From where he sat, he had only a limited view of the landscape. When he first heard the sound, he didn't know what it was, mechanical or insectoid. It was muffled by the cab. After a while he decided that it was mechanical, a vehicle. Without being able to see the source, he was unable to tell if it was nearing or moving away. Only after long straining intervals of suspense was he able to say that it was indeed nearing.

A blur of motion entered the narrow slice of landscape he could see. It was a gray-green Jeep, making straight for the trail, leaving a tail of dust.

Albert knuckled his eyes, rubbing away stinging

sweat, blinking, focusing blearily on the oncoming vehicle. He recognized it as a Jeep from Mr. Larry's ranch.

Albert could guess what had happened. Attention had been paid when he and Ralston had failed to deliver their human cargo. Mr. Larry had waited around for a while, long enough for Ralston and Albert to handle any unexpected glitches that might have thrown them off their timetable. Even if they had gotten busted, they'd have been able to make a phone call by now. So, when the deadline passed with no word of the missing, Mr. Larry had sent a couple of hands to investigate. Bender's Ford was the logical place to begin a search, and so now, in early afternoon, here came the searchers.

There were two of them in the Jeep, but Albert couldn't make out who they were, not yet. The Jeep was an open-top job. That worried him, but the machine kept rolling along, encountering nothing but empty air as it neared the top of the ridge.

In his first rush of excitement, he started to get out to meet them. He slid over to the passenger side and had his hand on the door handle, when something made him stop.

Buzzing.

Or was it? The sudden motion had made him dizzy, and he wasn't sure what he'd heard. The pulse beat echoing through his ears and into his skull made it impossible to hear anything else, momentarily drowning out even the thrum and rattle of the fast-approaching Jeep.

The wave of weakness passed, leaving him sitting in place.

He didn't see any bees, not a one. And he didn't hear any. Now that his thudding pulse beat had lessened, he could hear the oncoming Jeep, and only the Jeep. No buzzing.

Still, why take chances?

The Jeep crested the ridge, filling the mouth of the trail. If the riders hadn't been able to see the utility truck from below, they certainly couldn't miss seeing it now.

The Jeep bounced to a halt, just inside the tunnel in the green. It was only about thirty feet away. He could recognize the rider, Sherm, and the driver, Fournier.

They were pointing at the truck cab, peering at it, at him! They got out of the Jeep and started toward him. Albert was glad it was they who had come along first, instead of some outsider. He'd hate to have to explain what he was doing here to the Law.

Sherm and Fournier were cowboys and they walked like they had just climbed down off a horse. They were stiff and sore from the long rugged off-road trek.

"Albert! You okay, boy?" Sherm said.

"Where's Ralston?" said Fournier.

"What you doin' in that truck? Come on out—"

Suddenly the scene erupted. It was as if the trees and leaves and bushes had dissolved into atoms, exploding. It looked like a TV image breaking down into video snow, a blast of dots of color and motion.

Lurking just behind the surface of a steamy wooded landscape was a swarm of killer bees. As if activated by a single mind, a single will, they all broke from concealment at once, from hollow decaying logs, from the undersides of leafy boughs, from everywhere.

Sherm and Fournier were two figures caught in the heart of a howling black blizzard of bees. One of them was rolling around on the ground of the trail, the other fled blindly and got no more than a half-dozen paces before running smack into a tree. He fell down and rolled on the ground, too. Albert couldn't tell which was which, the swarm was too thick.

The swarm hit the two like a whirlwind of razor blades, ripping them.

Soon the only motion was that of the bees. The two figures were still, motionless under billowing blankets of bees.

That was one thing Mr. Larry had left out of his plans: bees. Killer bees.

STEPHANIE STUCK HER HEAD INSIDE THE administration office. "Pssst, Rita!"

Rita sat at the near end of a straight-backed wooden bench that ran along one of the office walls. "Hi, Steff."

"What're you doing here?"

"Waiting for Mr. Brock."

"Uh-oh," Stephanie said, after first making sure that nobody else was around.

"It's not what you think," Rita said, laughing. "I'm not in trouble or anything." She lowered her voice, glancing toward the closed door of the vice-principal's inner office.

"I have to get you-know-who's okay on an article I'm writing about the election for a special edition of the *Blade*," she said.

"I thought the new issue didn't come out till next month."

"This is a Founders' Day special, Steff. It's only going to be four pages long. We're going to print it up this afternoon, in time for the fund-raiser at the

drive-in tonight. The Boosters' Club is going to give them out tonight and tomorrow at the town square."

It was now a few minutes into sixth period, the next-to-the-last class of the day. The administration office was a large high-ceilinged room located on the ground floor of the building. A long aisle ran from the outer door to the opposite wall, which featured lots of windows half-covered with pull-down shades. On one side of the aisle was the wall with the long wooden bench on which Rita sat. On the opposite side was a chest-high dark brown wood partition topped by a wide counter. There was a swinging door in the partition, now closed. Beyond the barrier lay a clerical work area, with two desks, one for Miss Quigley, and the other for her assistant. Both women were away from their desks, called out of the office on various errands.

At the far end of the aisle opposite the outer door, in the same wall as the bench, was the vice-principal's office. The upper half of the door was made of frosted glass. Painted letters spelled out the words BENNETT BROCK, VICE-PRINCIPAL.

Light shone from behind the glass and the muffled sound of two voices speaking in earnest conversation filtered out. One of the voices was Brock's, the other belonged to an adult male. Rita could hear the voices rising and falling, but was unable to make out what they were saying.

The outer door was open wide. Stephanie stood in the hall, leaning into the office. The hall was empty, classes now being in session.

"He's going to check the article?" Stephanie said, her eyebrows raised. "I thought that was Miss Hunsecker's job. She's the faculty adviser to the *Blade*."

"I guess he wants everything to be just so for Founders' Day," Rita said.

"Chubb Wynant got it off to a great start."

"He's such an idiot."

"I've got a scoop for you. Chubb's in the auditorium, cleaning up the mess he made."

Rita shrugged. "What's news about that?"

"He's cleaning it with a toothbrush."

"That *is* news. It's probably the first time he's had such a utensil in his hands."

"Probably," Stephanie said. "Are you going to print it?"

"No."

"Why not?"

"It's not good for school spirit."

Stephanie snorted. "Who says so?"

Rita tilted her head toward Brock's office. "He will."

"Whatever happened to freedom of the press?"

"He happened."

"Hey, Rita, how'd you like Jean winning?"

"Not much, but better than if Tammi'd won."

"I'd have liked to have seen Tammi's face when she found out she'd lost."

"I did," Rita said.

"And?"

"She took it better than Lucy did. From the way Lucy was carrying on, you'd have thought that she was the candidate and Tammi was the campaign manager, instead of the other way around."

"Of course, now Jean will be more smug and stuck-up than ever."

"I doubt that's possible."

"And Caro will be more manic than ever."

"Now that's a frightening thought," Rita said.

Stirrings emanated from inside Brock's office, chairs being pushed back, bodies rising.

"Sounds like the meeting's breaking up," Rita said. "Don't let *him* catch you hanging around."

"I've got a hall pass," Stephanie said.

"Likewise. I've got study hall now, but I've got a pass from Miss Hunsecker to work on the *Blade*."

Shoe leather scuffled, behind Brock's door, shadowy man-shaped outlines looming up behind the frosted glass.

"Think I'll take off," Stephanie said. "Even though I've got a pass, I don't want to see *him*."

"I don't blame you."

"I was going to ask what you were doing after school, but I guess you'll be working on the paper."

"Yes, I'll be hanging around the *Blade* office for a couple of hours, until it's printed up."

"You're still going to the drive-in tonight, right?"

"Wouldn't miss it, Steff."

"We can see Jean get crowned."

"I'd like to crown her myself."

"Maybe Tammi will. Crown her, that is."

"Let's hope," Rita said. "But that's not why I'm going."

Stephanie smiled slyly. "I know why you're going."

"To see the movies, Steff, to see the movies."

"You won't see much of them, wrestling around in the backseat with Arch."

"I'll be in the front seat. It's Arch's car. You'll be in the backseat, with J.W. And I'm sure we'll all behave like ladies and gentlemen."

"Oh, I'm sure," Stephanie said, mocking. "It doesn't help that they look like a pair of models for a fashion-magazine ad for men's western wear."

"Except that they're the real thing. But don't let that country-boy act of theirs fool you. They're a couple of fast operators."

"I know."

"Why, Steff, you're blushing."

Stephanie had started to retort when the knob to Brock's office's door rattled, as if it was being turned from the inside.

Rita said quickly, "Let's meet after dinner—so we can hang out before the guys come to pick us up."

"Okay. Call me when you get home."

"I will, Steff. See you later."

"Bye." Stephanie hurried off down the hall, out of sight.

Brock's office door opened, a hand on the knob. The hand's owner had started to exit, then paused to say something to the other person in the room. The arm was visible up to the elbow, with the rest of its owner hidden behind the door frame. It was a man's arm, hairy, freckled, and sunburned. It could only belong to the visitor, whoever he was.

He was saying something and Rita caught a fragment of it, the words *killer bees,* immediately followed by Brock shushing him.

Rita slid down to the other end of the bench, nearer the door, so she could hear better.

"Now hold on, Stover," Brock said. "I know you're the expert from the Pest Control Bureau, but you haven't shown me any proof that young Martens was attacked by a killer bee!"

"I don't have any, Mr. Brock," said Stover. He

was soft-spoken and even-toned, particularly in comparison with Brock's raucousness. Brock was keeping his voice down, but it could still have been heard in the hall. Rita had to strain to hear Stover.

He said, "The insect that made the attack was destroyed without a trace, so there's no way to identify it. But everything else about the attack points to an AHB."

"AHB? What's that?"

"Africanized honeybee, Mr. Brock. That's the technical term for what's commonly known as 'killer bees.' "

"But you don't know for sure that a—what did you call it?—that an AHB was responsible for the attack."

"Well, no, I don't know for sure." Stover's tone implied the opposite, that he was mighty sure, but was too polite to come right out and say it.

"If it was an AHB, you've got a problem. I don't mean just you, Mr. Brock, I mean the whole town. Bees are social creatures. Where there's one, there's many."

"No killer-bee sightings have ever been made in this area. I know, because I checked on it, Stover."

"That's true. But there's been some sightings near to here. You don't have to get far out of town before you're in some wild country. And being so close to the border . . .

"It's a big country, Mr. Brock. The Border Patrol can't police the area, and our bureau doesn't have a fraction of their manpower and budget. We're just a subbranch of the state agriculture department.

"The back country is lawless. There's gunrunners, smugglers, vicious criminals. It's worth your

life to stumble across them alone, out in the middle of nowhere. Needless to say, that doesn't inspire our investigators to go too far off the beaten path. Another danger is the honest citizens, farmers and ranchers mostly, who live out in the boondocks. When they see a stranger prowling on their land, they're liable to assume he's up to no good, and shoot first. How're they supposed to know he's just an honest Pest Control man?"

"All you've said adds up to a lot of excuses for not doing your job, Stover."

"All I'm saying is that there's a heckuva lot of unknown territory out there in the back country. There's water and brush and that's what bees thrive on, including AHBs. For all we know, there could be swarms out there."

"Or nothing at all."

"Or nothing at all," Stover admitted. "But I'll tell you this: Everything I've read about the attack yesterday indicates an AHB. The report by the medics who treated Martens at the emergency room confirms it. I'd know for sure, one way or another, if I could see him, examine his wounds."

"Why don't you?"

"Funny thing about that," Stover said. "The patient walked out of the hospital sometime early this morning."

"Good. I'm glad to hear he made such a quick recovery."

"He wasn't exactly released. The doctors wanted to keep him over for observation. It wasn't so much his physical condition that concerned them, although that wasn't great. What worried them was his mental state."

"Bosh! Martens is a healthy, unimaginative youngster, almost backward. He's not the type for 'mental states.'"

"All I know is what the medics told me. They thought he was delusional."

"Preposterous."

"Not at all. Bee venom is poisonous. Sometimes it can derange a brain, driving the victim temporarily off his rocker," Stover said. "But he should turn up soon."

"What! You mean he's still missing?"

"Without a trace. But he shouldn't be hard to find. There can't be too many three-hundred-pound monsters walking around in broad daylight in nothing but a hospital gown."

"**M**ISSED ME," ALBERT SAID, TAUNTING THE
bees. He was going a little crazy from being trapped
in the cab so long.

The bees weren't hiding now. They were out in
force. The immediate area looked like someone
had unloaded a couple of dump truck–size loads of
bees on it. Most of them were crawling, on trees,
leaves, stones, blades of grass, and dead bodies.
The air was dark with their whirring, buzzing
forms, but there were even more on the ground,
many more.

They had stopped stinging long ago, maybe an
hour or so earlier, but they were still agitated.
Every time Albert moved, a couple of bees snapped
on the movement and bulleted straight for him,
only to bounce off the window. The first dozen
times it happened, he had been scared, but now
that he knew that they couldn't get at him, he was
getting used to it.

He'd outwait them. When Fournier and Sherm
failed to return, Mr. Larry would send out others to

investigate their disappearance. Sooner or later someone would escape alive, to spread the alarm and get help.

How long could a person live without water? A day, two? Probably not much more than two. How long would the bees stay in place? There's a question.

The bees more or less avoided the Jeep, which stood with its motor running, as it had done for the last ninety minutes or so, when Fournier and Sherm had first pulled up. Gray exhaust fumes putt-putted from the tailpipe. It would probably keep on idling until the gas ran out.

"With my luck, it'll get overheated and catch fire and burn everything up, me included," Albert said.

The bees didn't like the Jeep, with its ceaseless mechanical vibrations, its smells of hot metal, oil, and gas. They buzzed around it but pretty well kept clear of it. Those few bees who touched down on it quickly took to the air.

Suddenly the scene exploded, as before, when the bees had struck down the newcomers, only this time there were no newcomers, no moving targets to serve as a focus for the swarm's wrath, at least none that Albert could see. One instant the scene was as before, with the myriads of bees covering the brush in jeweled living armor, and the next, the swarm instantly took flight.

Albert was terrified that they had somehow figured out a way to get to him inside the cab, and they were making their final assault. Instead, the swarm spiraled up into the air and flew away.

They flew north, across the fields, a grainy swirling blob dwindling in the distance.

Albert forced a laugh. "Try to fool me! . . . I know what you're doing. You want to fool me into thinking you've gone away and it's safe to come out, and then you'll lower the boom.

"Well, forget it! I'm too smart to fall for that trick. I'm going to stay put and sit tight."

He stayed put and sat tight, but the swarm didn't come back. They were a blot no bigger than his hand on the hazy sky. The ridge formed one end of a long low saddle of land. In the distance, to the north, lay another low ridge, marking the opposite end of the saddle.

Behind the ridge rose a pale green cloud. The swarm flew into it and disappeared.

Albert began to tremble about five minutes after the swarm had gone. For the first time he began to wonder if they actually had quit the area, for whatever reason, not to return. That's when he began to tremble, at the possibility that he might be able to escape.

There were bees on the ground, dead ones. They'd died from exhaustion after their orgy of stinging, or lost their wings or been crushed by their fellows in the swarming mass.

Fournier and Sherm were there, too, now uncovered by the departed bees, their bodies revealed in all their stark horror. Albert tried not to look at them.

He tried to work up the nerve to make a break. Indecision was agony. At any moment the swarm might return. Or not. In the meantime his chances narrowed. If he waited long enough, the chance might be lost. Eventually—how soon?—the Jeep would run out of gas.

Doing something was better than thinking about it and doing nothing. Besides, there were no bees in sight.

"Talk about now or never!" Albert said to himself, groaning. He took a deep breath and made his move.

He opened the door, rolling out on the passenger side. Leaving the truck cab was like escaping from the tomb of a premature burial.

After long hours of confinement he was weak, his legs rubbery. But the fresh air acted like a tonic, keeping him on his feet. And the close-up sight of Fournier and Sherm gave him more incentive. They looked like two heaps of purple-red trash bags stuffed to overflowing.

The air was laced with a sharp tangy scent, the residue of the megadoses of bee venom that had been released.

Albert stumbled to the Jeep and tumbled into it. He heard stray hums zipping through the air. There were still a few straggling bees left in the woods, not many, but they were zeroing in on him.

He got the Jeep in gear, wrestling the steering wheel, backing up and turning around in the trail, brush crackling under the tires. Something swooped at his head. He hollered and ducked, and the bee missed on its first pass.

Then he had the Jeep pointed at the trail mouth and stepped on the gas. It catapulted forward, out of the woods and down the ridge.

Buzzing sounded behind him, so close that the back of his neck tingled. It wasn't the swarm, only a few dozen or so stragglers that were hot on his

trail. "Only" a few dozen. He remembered what one had done to Ox Martens.

He drove as fast as he dared, nearly overturning the Jeep a few times. The bees' top speed was anywhere from ten to fifteen miles per hour, and they couldn't keep flying all-out for too long. The Jeep was much faster, and inevitably pulled away, the whining buzz fading to a tinny drone.

Albert drove diagonally across the fields, northeast toward the highway. He drove hunched over, shoulders tensed in anticipation of a blow from above. He kept darting nervous glances skyward. He dreaded the return of the swarm. Now he knew how a baby chick feels when a hawk circles overhead.

The swarm had been drawn to the cloud of Green Mist. He would steer well clear of the stuff.

The needle on the gas gauge was nudging "empty." It wasn't there yet, not quite . . . but soon.

Not enough gas to make it into town. Maybe enough to make it to Mr. Larry's ranch, if the swarm wasn't cruising the highway.

He'd find out.

HUGO WAS ON THE ROOF, SPRAY GUN IN hand. It was four o'clock on Friday afternoon. Most of the students and faculty were long gone, getting a head start on the Founders' Day weekend. Not Hugo, though. Technically he was on duty for the next hour, until five o'clock. Trust Brock to hold him to it! Brock was on duty, too. His car was one of the few left in the faculty parking lot. From where he stood on the roof, Hugo could've spit on it. But he dared not. Brock would find him out.

Mr. High-and-Mighty Brock! He was in his office now, probably shuffling some paperwork around on his desk, but not before he'd made a point of collaring Hugo and demanding to know if he had checked the roof during his exhaustive, and exhausting, search for bees the day before. Hugo had to admit that he hadn't. Brock knew that, but he liked putting Hugo on the spot. He told Hugo to check the roof.

It was a dirty trick to pull, especially on Friday, as quitting time neared, but Hugo couldn't say no.

And of course Brock would stick around to make sure that Hugo complied with his request.

Brock wouldn't admit it, but Hugo could tell that the vice-principal had been upset by his talk with Ed Stover, the man from the Pest Control Bureau.

"He must've put a bee in Brock's bonnet," Hugo said to himself, grumbling. It was after his talk with Stover that Brock had hunted out Hugo and handed him the rooftop job.

It was a flat roof, like most of those in this arid land. On it was a boxcar-size air-conditioning unit. The roof bristled with square-sided ventilator housings and shiny aluminum conduit pipes.

In its center was a cabinlike structure with a small peaked roof. All four walls were solid, windowless. One had a metal door in it, now closed, which Hugo had used to get on the roof.

The air on the roof shimmered in the hazy sun. Hugo could feel its heat through the soles of his shoes. A breeze sighed, bringing too-brief relief.

Hugo smelled bananas. The sky overhead had a faint green cast. He glanced west, across the roof, to where the plant towered above the skyline. Sure enough, green smoke trailed out of the stacks, streaking southeast across the sky.

Hugo wrinkled his nose, rubbing it with the back of his hand. He turned, facing east. He stood in the shadow of the little stairwell house, a short stretch of rooftop between him and a skylight. Beyond the skylight lay a knot of ventilator shafts and pipes.

It was a mini-maze that looked like a good place to start looking for insect pests. Hugo trudged toward it, spray gun tucked under his arm like a shotgun. He passed the skylight, which opened on the gym. Two stories below, on the gym floor, a dozen members of the student Boosters' Club were working on decorations for tomorrow's Founders' Day festivities, to be held in the town square.

"If they like work so much, they can have this job," Hugo said.

When he got near the jumble of pipes and housings, the buzzing jarred him out of his thoughts and made him look up.

Under the overhanging top of a ventilator shaft, about eight feet above the roof, was a football-sized hive and about fifty thousand bees.

Oozing out into the open like thick clouds of oily smoke, the swarm formed a looming mass, towering ten feet above Hugo. He backed away, the useless spray gun falling from his nerveless fingers.

This was not the swarm from Bender's Ford. There was more than one killer-bee swarm in the area. Population pressures had caused this group to split off from the others, forming its own nest. They had built it only recently, here on the roof of Sibley High.

They came down on Hugo, a whirling buzz saw. He started to come apart, like he'd been dropped in a wood-chipping machine.

He fell backward, toppling onto and through the skylight. The greenhouselike structure of a metal framework and panes of reinforced glass imploded like a bomb burst under Hugo's weight.

The students working in the gym looked up in time to see Hugo fall, kicking and screaming, in a shower of metal struts and glass shards, cascading two stories down to hit the hardwood gym floor with a sickening *crunch*.

There were a few shouts and screams. Then the swarm flew in through the open skylight and the screaming really started.

A whirling column of killer bees corkscrewed into the gym, falling on the shrieking students, catching them up in a pitiless vortex.

There was more screaming and some running around, but no one made it out of the gym alive.

The gym was not all that far from the auditorium, where Chubb Wynant labored with a toothbrush and a bucket of soapy water scrubbing the wall. Long hours ago, even working with the brush, he'd cleaned up the entire area he'd egged. But that wasn't enough for Brock, who told him to keep on doing what he was doing until he was told to stop.

The clatter and shouts from the gym had come echoing through the walls, along the heating and cooling ducts. When he first heard the racket, Chubb made a sour face.

"Lousy rah-rahs, always finding some reason for yelling their heads off like a pack of blamed fools," he muttered.

He heard some more . . . and stopped what he was doing and listened hard. The sounds were coming through a wall-mounted heating grate. He pressed his face to the metal grille, listening to the echoing cries.

"Jeez, it sounds like somebody's getting murdered," he said, frowning.

A buzz rattled through the pipes, dense, angry, and churning.

"What is it, a chainsaw massacre?" Chubb said.

Then the buzzing grew louder and came faster, emanating from the piping duct straight at him.

Some instinct made him throw himself back from the grille, knocking over the pail and spilling soapy water across the stage apron.

An instant later a mob of bees roared out through the spaces in between the grille, hurtling into the auditorium like a shotgun blast.

An exit door was located near the end of the stage apron and Chubb dashed for it. He slipped on a patch of soapy water and fell. Before he got up, the bees were on him.

He didn't get up again.

Brock was sitting at his desk, behind a closed office door, but when the excitement started, he heard it loud and clear. There were stampings, crashings, shrieks, and howls. It sounded like a stampede in Hades.

The vice-principal jumped up, rigid, nostrils quivering. He was more outraged than if someone had insulted his mother. He crossed to the door, opening it, stepping into the outer office.

On the other side of the partition, in the work area, Miss Quigley stood staring at the door opening to the hallway, through which the atrocious sounds poured. Her eyes bulged and her mouth hung open. She seemed to have been frozen into immobility.

"Sounds like a pack of maniacs!" Brock said, churning down the aisle toward the door. "I'll soon set this right!"

Recovering from her paralysis, Miss Quigley pushed open the swinging partition half door and stepped into the aisle, falling in behind Brock, who was already out the door and into the hall.

A couple of members of the decorating committee had been outside the gym when the bees struck, but the swarm had them now. The students ran down the hall, screaming, trying to protect their heads with hands and arms, bouncing off the rows of lockers that lined both sides of the corridor.

Hanging overhead, like ghostly wraiths stretched out between the ceiling and the tops of the students' heads, was a mass of bees. They dropped down over the students, like a black veil. The students dropped, tumbling, rolling around on the floor, magnets for stinging buzzing bees.

When the students stopped moving, the swarm started toward Brock.

Brock turned, dashing into the administration office, running over Miss Quigley, who was in the way. He trampled her underfoot without mercy, leaving her for the bees. Perhaps that would slow them down long enough for him to escape.

The spearhead of the swarm came swooping in through the hall door. Brock was that all-important few paces ahead. He dove into his inner office, slamming the door behind him.

He slammed it so hard that the glass panel at the upper half of the door cracked in two. . . .

In the corridor, another door down, the reclusive Principal Twonky stuck his head out of his office to see what all the ruckus was about. Within seconds, a few hundred killer bees had fastened on his face, turning it into mush.

THE *BLADE* OFFICE WAS ON THE SECOND FLOOR, in a room that had once been a teachers' smoking lounge. But that was a long time ago. The room was in the building's north wing, facing west, toward the street. It was smaller than a classroom but bigger than a storeroom. Both the school newspaper and yearbook were put together here, often by the same student staffers.

There was a workstation, a personal computer with a laser printer, some filing cabinets, a desk, a table and some chairs, and a few odds and ends.

In the room was a teacher and four students. Miss Hunsecker, an English teacher, was faculty adviser to the student newspaper. Gladys Dinmont was the editor, Troy Appling was an assistant editor, and Rita was the lead reporter, in what passed for reporting on the *Blade*. Which wasn't much, since Brock wanted only positive "news" that would promote upbeat school spirit. But it was a good credit for her college résumé, and it also gave Rita the chance to use the computer for her own projects, so it was worth it, she guessed.

Also present was Ernie Anderson, who couldn't write a sentence, and could barely talk, but who was the only one who could make the printer work properly. It was working now, spitting out sheets of paper for the special Founders' Day issue of the *Blade,* to be given out tonight at the drive-in and tomorrow in the town square. Everything was humming along nicely.

Then the racket started. At first it was hard to hear, over the sound of the printer and the chattering student staff. It came from a long way off, from another part of the building on the ground floor.

When the action moved from the gym and auditorium to the main hall and the administration office, they could hear it thundering from below, the sound of bellowing and buzzing.

Miss Hunsecker and some of the others hurried into the hall to see what was happening. Miss Hunsecker frowned. She was the authority figure here, but whatever was happening on the first floor wasn't something she was eager to handle.

She twisted her face into an expression of almost imbecilic disbelief. "What's that awful noise . . . ?"

Shrieks buzzed up the empty stairwells. At the far end of the hall lay the north staircase. Miss Hunsecker went to it, her stupefaction growing with each step. Trailing her by a half-dozen paces was Gladys. Troy stood in the open doorway, watching them.

In the room, Rita sat at the monitor, inputting the last of her article. She looked over her shoulder toward the door, frowning at the disturbance.

Nearby, Ernie sat watching the printer, seemingly hypnotized by its smoothly running efficiency.

Miss Hunsecker stood on the landing, leaning over into the stairwell. Up from its depths floated a buzzing black column like smoke rising in a chimney.

Miss Hunsecker didn't know what it was until the bees were upon her. She threw her arms over her head, shimmying as if she were trying to jump out of her skin. The buzz cloud engulfed her, sucking her out of sight into the well.

The swarm stretched a limb down the hall. The head of it grazed Gladys, spinning her like a top. The limb curved back on itself, wrapping around her. She whirled out of this world, accompanied by the wail of her own piercing screams.

Always an opportunist, Troy Appling was already inside the room, closing the door, even before the swarm had brought down Gladys.

Rita jumped up and now stood at the door beside him, face pressed to the clear glass inset panel. Troy held the doorknob, pulling it shut with both hands. His feet were braced against the bottom of the door.

Ernie looked up from the printer, frowning. "What is it . . . ?" He had to speak loud to be heard over the screams coming from the hall.

"Bees, killer bees!" Troy cried.

Rita glanced around, noting with horror the half-inch space between the bottom of the door and the floor.

"They'll get in under the door! We've got to block it!" she said. Hanging on the back of a nearby chair, where Miss Hunsecker had left it earlier, was a

blazer jacket. Rita grabbed it and laid it along the bottom of the door, stuffing the fabric into the space.

Troy dropped to his knees to help. He accidentally jostled the doorknob, rattling it. The door had no lock, only a spring bolt that jiggled in the jamb. Before the door could pop open, Ernie grabbed the knob, pulling it shut.

"You almost opened it, you idiot!" he shouted.

"Don't call me an idiot, you idiot!" Troy said.

Outside, Gladys had stopped screaming. That was good, because it had been horrible to hear, but it was bad, because it meant that the bees had finished with her and were ready to move on to other targets.

Rita could hear them buzzing on the other side of the door as she finished stuffing the last of the fabric into the gap.

"It's finally happened," Ernie said solemnly. "They said it had to happen and now it's come, the day of the killer bees."

"What are we going to do?" Troy said.

"Not open the door," said Rita.

Ernie pointed a trembling finger at the inset glass panel, the other side of which was swarming with bees.

"Look, they're piling on!"

"It's okay, they can't get through," Rita said. "Can they?"

"Not unless some idiot opens it," Ernie said.

"Shut up! You're the idiot!" Troy said. "Can ᵗʰᵉy—can they break through the glass?"

"ᵈᵒn't think so," Rita said. A thought struck

her, and she turned around, facing inward. "The windows! Are any of them open?"

The bottom of her stomach stopped feeling like it was dropping when she saw that all the windows were closed. And solid—no cracked panes.

Incredible that on the other side of the glass, the sun shone and occasional cars drove lazily up and down the street fronting the school, oblivious to what was happening inside.

What *was* happening inside?

There was a crackling sound, then a deep humming buzz filled the room. Troy said, "They're inside!"

But they weren't, not yet. Ernie glanced at the wall-mounted speaker, the source of this particular electronic buzz.

"It's the intercom. Someone's firing up the public-address system," he said.

"Somebody else is in the building! They can get help!" Troy was frantic.

"How will they know we're here?" Rita said.

"We'll make so much noise, they'll have to hear us."

Ernie said, "That hasn't done much good so far."

"Shut up, idiot."

"You're the idiot."

"Both of you shut up," Rita said. "It sounds like somebody's getting ready to send a message over the intercom."

"Yes, here it comes!"

Bleep.

"This is Bennett Brock! Anyone who can hear my voice, please send help! We are under attack by

killer bees, and—oh, no! Lord help me! They're get-
ting in! They're—
    "AIIIIIIEEEEEEE!"
    Blat!
    Buzzzzzzzzzzzzzzzzzzzzzzzz.
    "That was Mr. Brock, signing off," Rita said.

TALEMATE.

The bees couldn't get in, and the humans couldn't get out. The weak point of the room was a grilled cooling and heating airduct. They could hear the bees buzzing around in the innards of the building. The three of them managed to wrestle a heavy filing cabinet flush against the wall, blocking the outlet, blocking the bees.

The door was blocked as well. There were bees in the hall, lots of them. Most of them seemed to be crowded on the glass viewplate. It was almost a solid panel of bees. They bristled with hostility and thwarted rage.

There were some outside, too, hovering around under the eaves, in the vines. Not many, just enough. Not enough to attract attention from passersby, but enough to thwart any attempt to escape through the windows, risking the drop to the lawn two stories below.

There were lights on in the room. The electricity still worked in the building. The prisoners had tried

blinking the lights on and off, to attract attention, but it hadn't worked. They tried shouting at passing cars, but they didn't dare open the windows for fear of the bees outside. The building was set far back from the street, too far to be heard or seen by anyone driving past.

"What about the computer?" Rita said. "You know computers, Ernie. Can't you use this one to call for outside help?"

"Not without a phone modem and some other stuff. It's down in Mr. Brock's office. He didn't want anyone to have unauthorized access to school computer lines."

"So that's out."

"Unless you want to go down to the office and get the stuff."

"No, thanks."

Troy ground his fist into his palm. "This can't last! We're sure to be missed, and somebody's bound to come along to investigate."

"The bees'll get them," Ernie said gloomily.

"You're a big fat help."

Rita said, "I must be missed already. My folks will be worried that I wasn't home for dinner."

"It's getting late," Troy said.

"It's dark outside," said Ernie.

"What time is it?"

"I don't know, Rita, my watch is broken," Troy said.

"Mine isn't."

"Well, good for you, dork."

"It's almost eight-thirty, Rita," Ernie said.

"Just think," Rita said. "In fifteen minutes, Queen Jean'll be trying on her crown for the crowd at the drive-in."

"Imagine if they knew what was going on here!" said Ernie.

"That wouldn't stop Jean," Rita said.

Five minutes of silence passed. At the plant, the stacks vented another cloud of Green Mist. The wind, which had been blowing to the southeast, had begun to blow to the south, then gradually southwest.

Like a stately airship, the green cloud followed the gentle tuggings of the wind.

Outside the door in the high school, the bees buzzed into a sudden frenzy. There was a flurry of activity as they took to the air, racing through corridors and down stairwells, blowing out of the building.

The trio rushed to the window. Darkness had come, street lamps were lit, but some light still glowed in the western sky.

The swarm was outlined against it as they streamed above the rooftops in a blurred grainy oval mass that looked like a grimy smear above the horizon.

"They're . . . gone." Rita was amazed. "I wonder why?"

"Who cares, as long as they're gone?" Troy muttered.

"Maybe they went to see the show," Ernie suggested.

"Could be," Rita said seriously. "They took off in the direction of the drive-in."

"That's what I'm going to do," Ernie said. "Take off out of here, just as fast as my legs can carry me."

"What're you going to do, genius, just open the door and waltz out of here?"

"You know a better way, Troy? What're you going to do, jump out the window?"

"I might."

Rita said, "I'll jump out of it myself, if I have to stay here another minute with you two."

"Did you look down? It's a long jump," Ernie said.

It *was* a long drop. Rita walked to the door, peering through the glass panel. "I don't see any bees. Or hear them . . . "

"I'm not going to be the first out of that door."

"Somebody's got to take the plunge, Troy."

Troy gestured sardonically toward the door. "Ladies first."

"Okay." She reached for the knob.

Troy started, lunging for her. "Don't open that door, Rita—"

She opened it. The bees were gone. "Let's get out of here!"

Lights were on in the hall. The trio made for the north stairs, steering as far as possible from Gladys' sprawling swollen form. Shocked, hushed, they hurried down the stairs, only to find Miss Hunsecker's corpse sprawled at a crazy angle at the bottom of the shaft.

Rita put a hand over her mouth, fought to keep from gagging. "Maybe we should have taken the window instead. . . ."

Troy pushed past, hitting the spring bar on the

exit door. It opened outward, on the north side of the building.

The trio fell out the door, into the night. They ran down the walkway into the street and kept on running. Sibley High loomed up behind them, a grim fortresslike structure, the School of Death (as the news media would call it later, during their lurid exploitation of the tragedy).

Ernie and Troy turned right, running north. Troy ran into traffic and was hit by a car; he was taken to the hospital with a broken leg. Ernie may still be running yet.

Rita turned south. She ran down the middle of the street, along the white center line. Her hair streamed behind her, her arms and legs worked, her racing feet pounded the pavement.

A pair of headlights swung around, pinning her in their glare. She froze, dazzled and dazed as the vehicle bore down on her. It stopped about ten feet away.

Rita's legs folded and she sat down, right in the middle of the street. She rubbed her face and ran her fingers through her hair.

Car doors opened, passengers got out. "Rita!"

It was Stephanie. With her were J. W. Burns and Arch Mokely. They hurried to Rita's side, helping her up, steadying her.

"We've been driving around for hours, looking for you," Stephanie said. "Are you okay? Rita, what happened?"

Rita pointed at the school. "They're dead!"

"*Dead?* Who's dead?"

"All of them, Steff—Miss Hunsecker, Gladys Dinmont, everyone who was inside after school, except

for me, Troy, and Ernie Anderson! They even killed Brock!"

"How? . . . Who? . . ."

"Bees," Rita said. "Killer bees!"

31

THE HIGHWAY DRIVE-IN MOVIE THEATER WAS
located south of town, on the west side of the highway. It was far enough away from town that the
city lights didn't interfere with the outdoor movie.
A onetime cow pasture, the space was now enclosed
by an eight-foot-tall solid wooden fence. There was
one entrance, facing the highway. One dirt road led
in, and another came out. At the entrance was a
gatehouse that served as a ticket booth.

On a spit of turf between the dirt roads, near the
highway, stood a signboard, an illuminated marquee. It read:

HIGHWAY DRIVE-IN
NOW PLAYING:
FRI-SAT-SUN
2 BIG MONSTER HITS!

PLUS FRI PRESHOW:
FOUNDERS' DAY FUN

"SEE THE STARS IN YOUR CARS"
AT HWY DRIVE-IN

A line of vehicles stretched along the dirt road at the entrance to the drive-in. The ticket sellers in the booth weren't too fast.

Inside the fence was a lot with an outdoor movie screen at one end. The screen was placed with its back to the highway so that distracted drivers peeking at the movie when they should be watching the road didn't have accidents.

In the middle of the lot was a concrete block-house. The end facing the screen housed a snack bar, and the rear area held the projection booth. The lot was rippled with rows of low ridges. The ridges fanned out from the blockhouse, like circles spreading across the surface of a pond into which a stone has been dropped. The ridged rows allowed the patrons to park their vehicles at an angle, giving them an unobstructed view of the screen. The ridges were dotted with metal posts, like parking-meter stands. Mounted to the stands were wired speakers, supplying the audio portion of the program. Given the state of present technology, the speakers could have been wireless, but then too many people would've tried to steal them. Tough cable cords kept these speakers from wandering.

There was a big crowd for the Friday-night double feature. The place charged by the carload, making it good budget entertainment for teens, people with big families, and others without a surplus of cash—a large majority of the local population.

The lot was filled with cars, pickup trucks, vans, etc. Some people had brought lawn chairs, setting them up beside their vehicles. Some had brought food and drink, picnicking under the stars. Knots of kids ran between the ridges, kicking up dust.

The show usually began at nine o'clock. It was now almost a quarter to nine. Grouped around the front of the snack bar was a bigger crowd than would normally be seen at this time. And that was saying something, since the drive-in did a big refreshment-stand business. The snack bar was bright and brassy. Working behind the counter were a couple of young people in white aprons, all relatives of the drive-in's owner. The griddle sizzled with frying burgers. Soggy french fries cooked in vats of bubbling grease. There was soda and soft drinks, popcorn and candy. For the nutritionally reckless, there were batter-dipped and fried corn dogs.

The lines were long. People liked to lay in their snacks before the movie. Plus, the service was slow, like at the ticket booth.

A special promotion had been set up over to one side of the snack bar. This was part of the Sibley High School annual Founders' Day fund-raising event. It was a tradition. Every year, Little James Pettigrew, the drive-in's owner, donated fifteen minutes of time to the high-schoolers. It was before the show, so it didn't cost him anything. If he'd tried to run it later, delaying the features, the patrons would probably have lynched him. Another tradition was his yearly donation of twenty-five dollars, to kick off the fund-raising. He didn't

like that so well, but it was the price you had to pay for good community relations, so he would grin and bear it.

Little James Pettigrew was setting up the microphone for the event. He was an adult with a full-grown son of his own, but he was known throughout the county as Little James, to distinguish him from his father, Big James. Big James had been dead for twenty years and more, but the drive-in's owner was still stuck with the name.

He was long-faced, with sunken cheeks and a bad toupee. An unlit cigarette dangled from his lips. He was dying for a smoke, but he figured it was bad for the drive-in's family image for him to be seen smoking around Sibley High's squeaky-clean teen princesses.

They were there, at the staging area, two knots of students representing the separate Jean and Tammi cliques. Jean wore a summery dress, white and pink, with a flaring bell skirt and a white waist sash flecked with silver specks. Her flawless face had never looked more beautiful, more doll-like.

At her side was the mercurial Caro, in a shiny pink dress with a scooped-out neck and back. Tonight, she seemed even more tightly strung than usual. One instant she was gloating; the next, anxious; the next, seething.

Although Caro showed it more openly, all the high-school seniors involved in the presentation were feeling the tension. All but Jean, it seemed, whose face was fixed in a mask of serenity.

What the students felt was more than the self-consciousness that often accompanies public speaking. They were worried. They kept looking around, searching the crowd for latecomers. There were urgent whispered conferences, followed by more worried looks.

Standing at one side were Jean, Caro, and three or four of their friends. Opposite them, at the other side of the presentation area, were Tammi, Lucy, and a handful of their friends. Between the competing cliques stood senior-class president Ken Fennel and two of his student-council stooges.

Tammi wore a red-and-black dress, Lucy wore green. Their group was enjoying the ever-growing discomfort of the Jean faction.

Massed around the presentation area was a group of around two hundred students, half of them Sibley students, and the others curious or at least tolerant bystanders. Most of the drive-in's patrons were a hometown crowd, and had gone to Sibley, so it was a friendly audience.

They were starting to grow restive, though, waiting for the presentation to begin.

Little James Pettigrew sidled over to Ken Fennel. He spoke out of the side of his mouth. "Better get the show on the road, kid."

"The others aren't here," Ken Fennel said. "We've got to wait for Mr. Brock and Miss Hunsecker and some other faculty members. And we're missing over half of the Boosters' Club. . . ."

"I thought you sent somebody to get them."

"I did. They should've been back a long time ago. I can't understand why they're not here. The school's only a ten-minute drive away."

"Call." Pettigrew gestured to a bank of pay phones.

"I've been calling for the last hour, but nobody's picking up at the other end."

"They must've left already."

"Then where *are* they?"

"How should I know?" Pettigrew was getting irked, but tried not to show it. "Look, kid, I'm sympathetic up to a point, but I'm running a business here. At nine o'clock, the show starts, no matter what."

"We can't start without the others—"

"Why not? It's no big deal. I'll come out and say a few words, make a pitch for your fund-raising drive. You and your friends come on and tell the folks to give for a worthy cause. It'll be short and sweet, and make everybody happy.

"Heck, nobody wants to listen to a bunch of dull speeches by the teachers anyway. They want to look at some pretty girls, and that's what they'll get. You'll probably raise more money this way."

"But we've only got half the Boosters, and they're the ones who go out into the crowd and collect the donations."

"You and the others in the presentation can join in. That'll make up the difference. Use some initiative, kid."

The crowd was growing impatient. Some of the more juvenile student types began to engage in horseplay, growing rowdy.

Ken Fennel fretted. Pettigrew said, "The natives are growing restless. Better do something, kid. This mike goes dead at nine sharp."

The other student presenters watched Ken Fennel, waiting to see what he'd do. He had to make a decision.

"All right, we'll go on," he said, mopping his sweaty forehead with a hanky.

The other presenters, Jean's and Tammi's cliques, formed up in a line behind the stand-mounted microphone. A cable ran from the base of the stand to an outlet somewhere inside the snack bar. A pair of PA speakers were mounted on the front corners of the snack bar's roof.

Standing beside Jean, Caro opened her handbag, taking out an object wrapped in tissue paper, like that used to wrap a corsage. The paper was violet-colored. Caro ceremoniously unwrapped it, peeling back the folds of paper to reveal a fragile silvery object that sparkled and glittered.

It was a tiara, a delicate chevron-shaped silvery web, decorated with rhinestones. It was the crown of Queen Javelina, a treasured Sibley High relic, which had been entrusted to Caro earlier that day, as part of her role as campaign manager of the winning candidate.

Its total worth was less than five dollars, but it had potent symbolic value.

This could be seen in the way Jean's eyes lit up when the crown was revealed, and in the hot-eyed covetous glances Tammi and, even more, Lucy cast its way.

Jean was aware of her rival's feelings, making her triumph all the sweeter. She took hold of the crown, balancing the delicate construct lightly in her hands, preparatory to putting it on her head now that the presentation was about to begin.

Bzzzzzzzzzzzzzzzzzzzzzzzzzzzzz . . .

A furious buzz sounded, rippling through the scene. People looked up, curious, annoyed, figuring

it was some kind of feedback squealing through the
PA system, which was far from state-of-the-art.

Then they looked up higher, into the sky, and
saw where the buzzing was really coming from.

The swarm began descending.

"ALBERT, PULL OVER!"

Albert kept driving. He was behind the wheel of the red car, rocketing north on the highway. Beside him, in the front seat, was Mr. Larry. In the back seat was Debra Gale.

Albert was worn to a frazzle and smelled bad, but he was in the best shape of the bunch. Mr. Larry was hurting. The bees had gotten to him. He was slumped in the corner of the seat, wedged against the cushions and the door. His bullet head was purple, his face swollen. His eyes were puffy slits, feverish looking. He breathed heavily through his mouth, sucking air, gasping. He'd taken over a dozen stings. He was puffed up with poisonous bee venom.

Debra Gale'd been stung a couple of times. She was sick and dizzy, but still full of fight.

Earlier, she'd almost run Albert down. She'd been driving then, wheeling the quick red car down the south highway. It was dusk. Albert was on the shoulder of the road, the northbound side, hiking

along. The Jeep had run out of gas a few miles back and he'd had to foot it. It was the dinner hour and there was little traffic. Even the truckers were chowing down somewhere at roadside cafés. A few cars and trucks had passed Albert, ignoring his frantic wavings and signalings for them to stop. One or two would have run him down if he hadn't gotten out of the way. He looked like a desert rat, crazy and maybe dangerous. Whatever, they kept on going. He kept on walking.

It was getting dark when the car appeared. Albert was nearing Mr. Larry's ranch, which lay over the next ridge, a half mile away. Then came the car, over the ridge and into view flashing down the south-bound lane. The headlights were dark and the car was weaving.

Albert stood in the road, waving his arms at the oncoming vehicle. It showed no sign of slowing and he moved out of its way. It wasn't until it had whooshed by and was dwindling down the road that he realized that it was his own car.

Red taillights had flashed as the car suddenly braked to a halt. It skidded and slid sideways to a stop. Albert ran toward it. When he was halfway there, the driver's-side door opened, but no one stepped out.

Then he was standing beside the car, peering down through the open door at Debra Gale in the driver's seat. She was trembling, glitter-eyed, her face flushed.

"A-Albert," she said, through chattering teeth. In the seat beside her was Mr. Larry. At first glance, he looked dead, but wasn't. He was hurting.

Albert got the story from Debra Gale. In late afternoon, a cloud of Green Mist had fallen on the ranch. It was a common occurrence, and no one gave it a second thought. Not long after, the bees struck. It must have been the same swarm from Bender's Ford, judging from the direction from which they had come when they blitzed the ranch.

It was like a rain of satanic imps, flying furies each armed with a white-hot nailgun stinger swollen with poison. They fell on the ranch like a divine judgment. Men, women, children, animals, anything that moved that was not of the swarm was targeted for stinging destruction.

Albert's car was quick and near, and he had left the keys behind for safekeeping before leaving with Ralston. Debra Gale and Mr. Larry had raced to the red car as the bees attacked. She was in the car before she noticed that he wasn't with her. He'd fallen, and was rolling around on the ground, being stung. She started the car and backed up beside him. When he'd managed to drag himself into the car, a few bees got inside with him, stinging Debra a few times before she was able to kill them.

They'd made their getaway in the red car, leaving behind a barnyard littered with dead and dying humans and animals, living pincushions for mindlessly hostile killer bees.

A limb of the swarm hovered north of the ranch, above the highway, so the red car had gone south. The venom was getting to Debra, and she was having trouble driving. When she'd first glimpsed Albert standing in the road, she thought she was hallucinating. But Mr. Larry rasped that he'd seen him, too, so she'd stopped the car down the road and here he was. And just in time, too. She knew

she wouldn't be able to drive much longer. Mr. Larry was in bad shape. He needed to get to an emergency room.

South, there was . . . nothing. Not even an area where they could get to some pay phones to call an alert to the town. Help, shelter, hospital, all lay north, in town.

Albert took the wheel and turned around, pointing north. The shortest distance between two points wasn't necessarily the highway, not when there were killer-bee swarms ahead on the prowl. Albert wasn't going to drive into any swarms. He remembered the hideous sight of hordes of them smearing themselves against the utility truck's windshield, blotting out his view and causing the truck to crash.

He had to make some lengthy detours to avoid the swarm. Now, at about a quarter to nine, he was back on track, once again heading north on the highway.

Ahead, in the distance, the glow of city lights showed over the horizon. Nearer were the lights of a gas station and, on the other side of the road, the lit-up marquee of the drive-in movie theater, and the lights of the cars waiting in line outside the entrance.

There was traffic on both sides of the highway. This close to town, stoplights had been set up at the crossroads. Albert slowed.

"I smell bananas," he said. And that was despite the fact that the car's windows were closed.

He ducked his head, looking up through the top of the windshield at the open sky. The moon had risen and shed a lot of light. Overhead, a cloud of

Green Mist began drizzling down on the scene, set-tling to earth.

Not one but two grainy black swirls fluttered above in the night sky, closing in on the green cloud from different directions. The Bender's Ford swarm, which had also hit the ranch and other lo-cales farther up the line, arrowed in from the southeast.

The second swarm, which had mauled Sibley High School, swept down from the northeast.

The two swarms met and merged in the sky above the drive-in, forming wheels within wheels, way up in the middle of the air. Like a descending blimp, the oval cloud dropped down on the drive-in movie, their whirling buzzsaw motion shredding the green cloud into thin banana-scented wisps fluttering to the ground.

Traffic on the highway had come to a halt, dri-vers pausing to crane their heads out of car win-dows and look up, observing what appeared to be a curious aerial phenomenon.

Only a few, such as the three in the red car, knew what they were seeing. They kept their windows rolled up.

The crowd outside the drive-in snack bar looked up as the swarm descended. The crowd dispersed, separating into its component parts. Everybody ran, scattering. It was save yourself if you can.

A number of people got trampled in the first mad rush. They were ripe pickings for the swarm, but all humans were prey. The swarm fell on the crowd like a lawn mower on grass. If grass had ears, per-haps the last sound it heard, as the whirring rotary blades descended, would sound like the buzz of the

swarm sounded to the screaming doomed humans as they were taken up by the killer-bee whirlwind.

Everyone ran every which way, in mad panic. Something glittered on the ground, catching Lucy's eye. The tiara crown! Jean must have dropped it when she fled. Neither Jean nor Tammi was in sight.

Lucy snatched up the tiara. The crowd was running away from the snack bar. Lucy did the opposite. She went into it.

Her taking of the crown had not gone unnoticed. Caro huddled nearby, taking cover, unobserved. Her eyes had widened, then narrowed, as Lucy picked up the tiara.

She followed Lucy into the snack bar.

The drive-in movie lot was chaos, pandemonium. People fled between rows of cars, screaming as strands of bees ribboned down on them. The swarm buzzed. Vehicles started up, headlight beams lancing across the darkness. Most of the vehicles had their windows open. The bees flew right in.

Cars crashed into each other. Headlights broke, crunching. Fenders crumpled. People were run over. Horns blared, especially when they were wedged into place by drivers who dropped dead from bee stings, collapsing across the wheel.

There was a chain reaction of crashes. Always, the bees were there, exploiting any opening, any shattered window or torn metal, to get at the meaty flesh puppets trapped inside the metal shells. Not to eat, but to rend them, stinging, destroying.

People fleeing on foot sought shelter in cars, but the owners were rarely obliging. Some died beating with ever-weakening fists against the side of a locked car while its occupants cowered within. Others threw open doors, allowing bees to get at one and all.

A limb of the swarm swirled into the snack bar, wrapping around a white-aproned girl behind the counter. She thrashed blindly, falling on the griddle. She screamed, flopping to the floor behind the counter. Bees followed her down, and she didn't get up.

A surprisingly nimble fat boy shimmied out from behind the counter and plunged into a side passage. He looked like he knew where he was going, so Lucy followed him. Caro followed her.

The fat boy ducked into a back room at the end of the passage. He started to close the door. Lucy straight-armed it, hitting it with the heel of her palm. The door sprang open, hitting its leading edge against the fat boy's forehead. His eyes rolled up, and he flopped back, stunned.

The bees were right behind Caro as she slipped into the storeroom, right behind Lucy. In the passage was an older woman, also making for the storeroom. The bees were on her, veiling her head. She beat at them, shrieking, running at the door.

Caro slammed it shut, closing it in the woman's face, which the bees were already starting to demolish. Caro leaned against the door with all her weight. When Lucy realized what Caro was doing, she joined her.

The two stood side by side, backs braced against the door, holding it closed. Outside, the woman hammered at the door, fists thudding against the panels, screaming to be let in. In her desperation,

she almost forced it open, but Lucy and Caro dug in and held it closed.

Lucy noticed a bolt mounted on the door and slid it into place. The bolted door was secure. The hand with which Lucy had done the bolting still clutched the crown, which was crumpled, soiled, and shedding rhinestones.

"Give it to me," Caro said.

Lucy laughed. Caro grabbed for the crown, and Lucy fended her off. They started fighting, tearing at each other.

Bees flew in under the door, fastening on the two battlers. Lucy and Caro kept fighting, trying to kill each other.

Meanwhile the fat boy came to. When he saw the girls fighting, he cried, "Are you crazy?"

Now that he was moving and making noise, the bees went after him, too. More bees flew in under the door.

33

A CAR DROVE OUT OF THE DRIVE-IN. NOT BY the exit, but by crashing straight through the wooden wall fence. It was mostly plywood, so it was pretty easy to destroy. Other cars tried it, some crashing into each other in the process.

Traffic was moving again, drivers stung by panic. The swarm touched down on some cars on the highway. Vehicles began leaving the road and driving into the fields to escape.

Ahead, in the northbound lane, was a gas station. Parked near the pumps was a fuel tanker truck. Trailing from its rear was a hose the size of an elephant's trunk, its nozzle screwed to the surface valve of a belowground fuel storage tank.

Mr. Larry stirred. "Pull into that gas station, Albert."

Albert looked at him sideways. "What for?"

"Pull over!"

Even in his weakened condition, Mr. Larry wasn't much for explanations. He was an action man. He

grabbed the steering wheel and turned it toward the right.

The car swerved. Albert said, "What're you doing—"

The gas station was approaching fast. A couple of uniformed attendants and some customers were standing outside, staring at the drive-in. They saw the car coming at them and they scattered.

A gas pump was coming up edgewise at the windshield, until Albert got control of the wheel and swerved to avoid it. He braked to a halt.

Mr. Larry shouldered open the door, swinging his big feet on to the pavement and rolling out of the car. He moved like a bear walking upright on its hind legs, staggering toward the driver's side of the cab of the fuel truck.

Albert got out of the car and stood beside it, watching as Mr. Larry fumbled open the door and started trying to climb into the cab.

"Hey!" The fuel-truck driver saw what was happening and ran over, grabbing Mr. Larry. "What do you think you're doing!"

He got a good look at Mr. Larry's face, all purple and swollen, and fell silent, gaping. While he was standing there with his mouth hanging open, Mr. Larry decked him with a punch to the head. It was sloppy and off balance, but there was plenty of weight and power behind it and the trucker went down, sitting down hard on the pavement, dazed.

Mr. Larry clambered up into the cab and sagged into the driver's seat. He started the engine and threw it into gear and drove away. The hose tore loose from the nozzle, spurting streams of gasoline behind it.

The fuel truck angled out of the station lot and started across the highway. Other cars got out of its way.

"Maniac! What's he doing?" Albert shouted.

"They've done for him," Debra Gale said tiredly. "Now he's going to do for them. He's a hard man, that Mr. Larry, a hard unforgiving man."

"He's going to kill innocent people!"

"It's a good thing he's not here, Albert. He'd kick your behind if he heard that softie talk."

Driving south toward the drive-in was Sheriff Lloyd Dell, two deputies, and the man from the Pest Control Bureau, Ed Stover. One of the deputies was driving.

"I didn't know what it was before, but I do now," Stover began, leaning forward in the backseat of the speeding patrol car. "It's the gaseous factory by-product that you call Green Mist. It's an organic substance. I won't know for sure until later, after an analysis, but it's my guess that the stuff is chemically similar to the bee's attack pheromone.

"Pheromone—it's kind of a hormone, only outside the bee. When they smell one, they react. During an attack they give off a certain pheromone. It makes them keep on attacking, stinging until the victim is dead, and sometimes after. I'm speaking specifically now of AHBs—killer bees, to you.

"I think that Green Mist is nearly identical to the killer bees' attack scent. I think that's what brought the swarms here in the first place, as well as what causes them to attack with such ferocity, even for them."

Dell said, "How come it never happened before, Stover?"

"The AHBs were never here before, Sheriff. It wasn't until now that their species' northward migration took them this deep into Texas. Now they're here, and you see the result."

"Why didn't the stuff do the same to the local bees, turning them into killers. It's never happened, in all the years there's been Green Mist."

"Pheromones are very specific things, Sheriff. They fit their receptors like a key fits a lock. Green Mist is only keyed in to the AHBs. It doesn't work on domestic honeybees.

"Now that we know about the effect of Green Mist on AHBs, we can use it to get a handle on the problem. Possibly use it as an attractant to lure the swarms to their death."

"I'm glad to hear that, Stover, because the way things are going, pretty soon there's not going to be any town left—

"LOOK OUT!"

Dell shouted as a fuel truck crossed in front of them, plowing across the highway at right angles. The patrol car skidded, narrowly missing a collision with the rear of the truck.

"Madman!" Dell yelled.

The truck barreled across the field, toward the drive-in. It crashed through the wall, into the lot.

The swarm hovered around the concrete blockhouse like an atomic mushroom cloud.

Mr. Larry steered the truck straight toward it. A choking cloud of killer bees was sucked into the cab. Mr. Larry held the course, driving straight into the snack bar, through windows and walls.

Inferno.

A pillar of fire rose, incinerating the heart and core of the stricken swarm, vaporizing them.

Standing on the roadside, a safe distance away, was a gray car. Grouped around it were Mokely, Burns, Stephanie, and Rita.

The fire column bathed the scene in eerie orange light. It speared skyward.

"Reckon there's no hurry about paying those class dues now, Arch."

"Reckon not, J.W."

Stephanie said, "What're you, a pair of ghouls?"

A drunk wandered out of an alley where he'd passed out hours before, missing the entire cataclysm. He goggled at the chaos down the road.

"Must be some show at the drive-in," he said. "What's playing?"

" 'Bee-zarre,' " Rita told him.